RESCUE DOGS

DOGS

EMBER

RESCUE DOGS

EMBER

JANE B. MASON
AND SARAH HINES STEPHENS

Scholastic Inc.

ISBN 978-1-338-36202-2

10 9 8 7 6 5 4 3 2   19 20 21 22 23

Printed in the U.S.A. 40
First printing 2019

Book design by Stephanie Yang

For dog heroes and their people

01

The little yellow puppy wriggled in a heap with her littermates. She freed a tiny paw, twisted, and pushed her fuzzy snout underneath her brother's chin. She wanted to snuggle back to sleep. It was dark under the house where the puppies dozed, always. Even during the day. But she could not settle. Something was different. Something was wrong.

Struggling out of the pile, she stood on wobbly legs. She opened her eyes to peer into the darkness and blinked. The small puppy had only had her eyes open for a week, and she loved to gaze at dust mites, her littermates' floppy tails, and the slow-moving spiders that lurked in the murky dark of the den. But this dark was different from the dark she knew. This dark wasn't the cozy, warm dark that was good for napping and rolling around with her siblings. This dark smelled strange. It felt hot. And it burned her open eyes. She let out a yip and then stood still, waiting to feel her mother's comforting lick.

It didn't come.

The pup lifted her short snout and sniffed again. Even in the strange, thick air, she could scent it. Her mother was gone.

The puppies' mother rarely left the nest she'd made for her litter. When she did, she was never away for long—just long enough to get food or water or go to the bathroom. The yellow puppy yipped once more. She pricked up her floppy ears, listening for her mama to call back in return. All she heard were strange new noises—loud thumps, scrapes, snaps, and pops. Added to the smells, the sounds made her uncomfortable. A whimper rose in her throat. She swallowed, then let her mouth fall open as she strained to see and hear and smell more.

At last she heard her mother's bark, but that, too, was strange. There was a warning in it, a plea, and an urgency she'd never heard before. It also sounded muffled, as if it was coming from far away.

The puppy yipped back to her mom, though it was useless. Her tiny bark was swallowed up by the new noises. But that didn't stop her. She yipped again and again, waking her brothers and sisters. The other puppies joined in the cry. They struggled to their feet in turn and began yelping and yapping, adding their tiny barks to the din, calling to their mother.

It was not enough.

Stumbling around in the dark, the yellow puppy kept barking as she searched for a way out.

None of the puppies had ever been out of the nest where they'd been born. Their mama dog provided all they needed—food, shelter, comfort. They had never needed to know the way out. "Out" was a place they thought they might follow their mother one day. Now, suddenly, "out" was a place they needed to find right away.

The yellow puppy kept sniffing for an escape, searching for fresh air. The strange-smelling air stung her nose, and the strong scent was growing stronger every second. Soon it overwhelmed everything else. The little dog stopped. She could not trust her nose. She held still and focused on the sounds coming from all around her. She heard her mother's muffled bark, her siblings' cries, and other voices, too—human voices. One of them was deep and booming . . . louder than the others.

"Wait. The dog. She's trying to tell us something!" the voice bellowed from somewhere above her.

"Marcus, we've got to get out of here. I don't think the roof is going to hold. Grab that dog and let's go!"

"No. Wait," the booming voice repeated. "See her pacing? She keeps going back to that spot. There's something down there. And look at her belly. I think she has puppies!"

The yellow puppy yipped in the dark and tilted her head. New noises came from above: more thumping, and then a strange scratching sound.

"Stand back. Hold the dog!" the deep voice boomed. The scratching was replaced by a loud *WHACK*. Then another. And another. *WHACK! WHACK!*

The rest of the frightened puppies cowered together. The whole den shook. The yellow pup stood apart. She listened to the sound of splintering wood and a strange wailing creak as one of the floorboards that made the roof of the puppies' den was pried up.

A hazy shaft of light flickered into the darkness, and the yellow puppy heard the booming voice again—louder this time.

"Here!" it shouted.

The terrified litter moved farther into a gloomy corner as a large covered hand reached through the opening, accompanied by a thick cloud of gray smoke.

The gloved hand groped in the darkness, searching, as more and more smoke poured in.

The little yellow puppy had never been close to humans before, but she sensed two things: Danger was closing in, and help was near. Circling the rest of her litter, she nudged them with her nose toward the hand that grasped each one gently and lifted them out one at a time.

The yellow pup kept herding the litter to safety, ignoring the burning in her throat and eyes. Smoke filled her lungs. She struggled to breathe. She coughed as she pushed a brown puppy, the last one, forward and watched him disappear through the rough opening.

"We've got to get out of here, NOW!" the second voice shouted above her.

"I think there's one more!" the booming voice shouted back.

The gloved hand reappeared, and the yellow pup staggered toward it. Her vision grew hazy. Then, just above her, she heard a loud crack. Something split. A dark shape dropped down into the den behind her and glowing embers rained all around, lighting up the darkness even more and singeing the tiny dog's fur.

The pup yelped.

The hand disappeared.

And everything went black.

02

Something or someone covered the small yellow puppy's muzzle and pushed air into her lungs. She squeaked and sputtered as she exhaled.

"Come on, little Ember!" The puppy recognized the booming voice from before, only now it was a low, soothing rumble. "Come on," it coaxed. The little dog's eyes fluttered open, and she coughed. She was outside, wrapped in the huge hand of the man with the booming voice. The air was clearer, though the smell of smoke was everywhere. Lights flashed in the darkness. There were lots of voices.

"There you go!" the man rumbled. He gently rubbed her chest with his thumb as he cradled her. His hand was so big the little dog fit comfortably in the palm of his fire glove.

The puppy looked past the fingers to her first glimpse of the world outside her nest. Large vehicles with bright lights surrounded them. More humans stood around in small clusters, looking at what was left of the still-smoldering building. Some of them held hoses and sprayed water, which sent up plumes of smoke and steam. The little dog looked down to see her mother and littermates. They were lying on a cloth on the ground. A woman knelt beside them.

"You're going to be okay," the man said. He moved her closer to his hairless face, so close she could feel the warmth coming from his dark skin. She coughed again and squirmed. She was not uncomfortable, only curious. She wanted to see what was happening. She wanted to know who these people were and what they were doing. She wanted to know everything!

She sat up in the glove and other nearby human voices laughed and cheered. They were happy she'd made it out of the choking darkness, too. She stretched out her neck to give the gentle man who pulled her out a lick. He had given her back her breath, and this was a thank-you. Her tiny tongue found the small dent on the side of his cheek that appeared when he smiled. He tasted like the thick air and salt and something piney. He laughed. A happy rumble. She licked him again.

Marcus Riley held the puppy gently and gazed at her with his big brown eyes while Greta, one of his coworkers, checked the burn on the puppy's back. The little dog's golden-yellow coat seemed to glow, even beneath the soot and ash that covered her. Marcus smiled. The pup should have been trembling, terrified. Instead, her eyes glinted with mischief or curiosity . . . or both. She didn't flinch, even when Greta flushed the burn between her shoulder blades with water, dabbed it off, and placed a clean bandage over it. "You're a glowing little Ember, all right," Marcus chuckled. He accepted another kiss on his nose.

"Oooh! I think she's in love, Marcus!" Victor, one of the other firefighters, hooted. Marcus looked into Ember's smaller brown eyes and smiled. Yes, he supposed he might be a little in love, too.

"Looks like somebody might be taking home a new dog," Greta teased. She elbowed her coworker before packing up the first aid equipment. Marcus grinned and watched the little puppy in his hand chew and tug on the thumb of his glove. She was sweet. And determined and unflappable. She'd nearly died, and here she was tussling with his thumb. She was a good dog, for sure.

But Marcus's smile disappeared when he thought of his own dog at home. Sadie. She was a good dog, too, and Marcus's best canine friend. Her puppy days were well behind her—they had been together since Marcus was a boy. Sadie was old and a bit frail, and would be insulted by a new puppy . . . even one with floppy ears, a twinkle in her eye, and a diamond-shaped burn on the back of her neck. No. He could not bring this puppy home. He couldn't do that to his Sadie.

"You're too little to leave your mama," Marcus said softly to Ember. "Besides, they'll be able to find you a good home at the shelter. That's where people go to find dogs. Someone will definitely want you."

Ember looked at the man. She didn't know what he was talking about, but she liked his voice. And she liked his glove. She liked to bite it! It felt good on her itchy puppy teeth.

"Oh, would you look at that." The owner of the burned house walked over to the firefighters and dogs. Her gray hair was in disarray, and she had a lost look about her that Marcus had seen before. She seemed shocked. Losing your home to flames was hard to grasp.

The woman peered at the puppy in Marcus's hand,

and her own hands flew to her mouth as tears filled her eyes. Her house was gutted. She'd lost nearly everything. And yet lives had been spared. Even this tiny new life in the firefighter's hand. "I'm so glad those dogs are safe," she said. "I had no idea they were living under the house! They could have been trapped, or . . ."

Greta, who was done packing up supplies, kneeled back down to pet the mama dog and the wiggly puppies squirming all around her, trying to nurse. "They were probably living under your back hall for a while," she explained to the woman gently. "I'd say these puppies are around three weeks old."

"I had no idea," the woman repeated, shaking her head.

"How would you have known?" Greta asked soothingly. She raised a hand to wave over a man in an Animal Services uniform. She'd called Animal Services as soon as she realized that the dogs were going to need shelter.

"I wish I could keep them," the woman said, sniffling, "but I'm not even sure where *I'm* going to end up af . . . after . . ." Her eyes welled with fresh tears, and she looked from the dogs to her house. A few firefighters were still soaking hot spots, and her voice trailed off.

"We'll take care of the dogs," the Animal Services man reassured her. He was experienced at assessing a scene and getting right to work. He patted the homeowner's shoulder before kneeling down by the Labrador and her litter. "You don't need to worry. These puppers are going to be just fine."

"Here, Mama." The worker offered the mother dog a treat, which she took gratefully. Then he put a second treat in the open crate he'd brought with him and placed nearby. "More inside," he said, and patted the big carrier box. Ember's mom stood wearily and walked inside, her puppies bumbling along at her heels. "There you go." The worker smiled. He glanced up at Marcus, who was still holding the yellow puppy. "Is that one yours?" he asked.

"Afraid not." Marcus was surprised to feel a little lump in his throat as he said it. He swallowed and bent his neck to touch his nose to the dog's tiny muzzle. "Take care, little Ember," he whispered into her floppy ear. He squatted down and placed her gently in the crate with her family, slipping off his glove to stroke her soft fur. Then, without really thinking, he tucked his glove in beside her so she could keep chewing on the way to the shelter. Ember looked up at the nice man before snuggling in with her brothers and her sisters and her chewy new glove.

03

One year later . . .

The car rolled to a stop, and Ember heard the lady behind the wheel, Nancy, let out a loud sigh. "Here we go," she said. It sounded like she was talking to Ember, but she wasn't. She didn't really talk to Ember unless she was yelling. Yelling at Ember was something Nancy did almost every day.

The tailgate of the car opened, and Ember jumped down, happy to be out of the rolling metal box. She didn't love riding in cars, but she did love to explore new places. The parking lot didn't have much to offer. But . . .

She filled her nose and made a beeline toward the smell of dogs. Lots of dogs! She was caught short when she came to the end of her leash. It choked her.

"Stop pulling!" Nancy yelled.

Ember leaned toward the base of the sign— the spot the dog smell was wafting from. Then she caught another scent. The shrubs on the edge of the lot smelled of dog, too! Maybe she would be allowed to go *that* way. Ember bolted in the other direction. She'd gotten bigger in the last year . . . much bigger! She was still lean, but her legs were longer and she moved faster. And she didn't always remember her own strength. She started to run across the parking lot and was choked to a halt. There was more yelling, and Ember looked around, trying again to figure out which way she was allowed to go.

"You don't listen," Nancy hollered, following her. "That's why . . . you . . . can't . . . stay!" she puffed.

Stay. That was a word Ember had heard before—a word she knew. She stopped. Sat. Stayed. And Nancy almost fell on top of her.

"Oh, come on!" Nancy let out another exasperated breath and tugged Ember toward the swinging door of Arroyo Animal Services. Ember hadn't recognized the place from the outside, but when she heard the bell over the door jangle and her feet hit the cool linoleum floor, it all came flooding back. This was the place she had come with her mother and litter-mates after their den caught fire. This was the place she kept returning to.

It was here that she had watched each of her brothers and sisters get picked up and cooed over and cuddled. Where people chose them and took them home. Ember was picked and cuddled and taken away, too, after everyone else, even the puppies' mother. And then she had come back again. And again. And again.

Ember liked the old man who had adopted her first. He took her to his tall, tall house. He liked to give her treats and to stare at a flickering screen with her lying beside him. He knew how to scratch the spot behind her ears. Sometimes they went on walks, but not enough. Ember wanted to be outside. Outside there were smells and things to see and chase and taste. The old man liked the outside best when he was on the other side of the glass, looking at it without smelling or feeling it.

Being inside all the time made Ember anxious. The screen bored her. She sniffed around the apartment and *pretended* she was outside. She chewed the furniture like sticks. She dug the rug like it was dirt. She peed on the couch like it was a tree. The man rolled up newspapers and swatted her to make her stop. She couldn't stop, though. So the man brought her back. "She needs someone more active," he said kindly. "She has so much energy."

The next family that took Ember home had a baby who walked in a funny, wobbly way. They were nice and let Ember eat the food the baby threw on the floor. They also made her stay on the other side of a fence in the house so she would not bump the baby and tip her over. And they made her sleep by the washing machine, where the ground was cold and damp, even through the old towels they laid down for her. She was lonely for her mother and brothers and sisters. She longed to sleep in a heap. She was so lonely she cried. She was so lonely she ate the shoes by the back door.

"A toddler and a puppy at the same time is just too much," the family had said sadly when they returned her. The mom couldn't look at Ember. The dad patted her head.

The baby waved over her mother's shoulder as they left. "Bye, bye, bye," she'd burbled.

Ember's head drooped. Yes, she remembered this place. It was the place animals came to find their "forever homes." Only Ember's homes hadn't been forever. Not once.

"We tried," Nancy said to the woman at the desk. "Lessons. Books. Everything. It's just not working out. I don't know if this dog is trainable." Her voice was high-pitched and tight. She smelled frustrated.

Ember's head drooped even lower.

"Oh, Ember." When she heard her voice, Ember remembered the woman behind the desk. Her name was Jo. She had a long black ponytail. She whistled when she was thinking about things, and she usually had a hopeful note in her voice that Ember loved. Today that note was gone. Today she sounded sad, and there was no whistling.

Nancy held Ember's leash out to Jo, who stepped around the desk to take it. The door jangled as Nancy went back through it without saying goodbye. Jo kneeled down beside Ember. She lifted the dog's chin. "What are we going to do with you?" she asked. "That's strike three. We're running out of options."

Ember wagged her tail slowly. She hoped it would bring back Jo's hopeful voice.

Both of them started when the bell over the door rang out again. "I almost forgot. You should take these. For Ember, or whatever." Nancy plopped down a box full of well-worn dog toys. Ember could smell her favorite chew glove on top and wagged a little faster. She was glad Nancy hadn't forgotten.

"Whoa, what's all this?" Jo asked, pulling her pony-tail over one shoulder and looking into the box.

"Ember found those. All of them. They were in our backyard. Apparently someone else had a dog there years and years ago. We had no idea."

Ember lifted her nose and sniffed. The smell of her favorite toy and all her found treasures filled her snout. She had sniffed and dug and discovered each and every one. She'd spent hours and hours in the backyard, locked outside alone. Each time she located a new treat, she gave it to her family. She thought it might make them happy. It only made them mad. It only made them yell even more.

Jo let out a little laugh of disbelief. She dug around in the box. "All of them?"

Nancy nodded. "Yes, except that nasty glove. She came with that and dug it out of the garbage every time I tried to throw it away. You should see our backyard. There are so many holes it looks like the surface of the moon! Apparently the last dog who lived there liked to bury things, and *this* dog liked to dig them up. Our lawn is toast."

"Oh, Ember." Jo sighed again as the door jangled for the last time. Ember wasn't sad to see Nancy go, but she was sad to be back . . . sad to not have a forever home.

Slowly, Jo led Ember out to the kennels, where the other dogs who were waiting for homes barked or slept or stared through the fencing and dreamed of open fields. Jo opened a clean kennel and patted the bed there. She checked the water and tossed Ember the chewed-up glove she'd pulled from the box. She'd almost forgotten about Ember's chew glove. It was such an odd toy, but the young pup was definitely devoted to it. "Can't believe you still have that," she said with a sly smile.

Then Jo got a look in her eye that Ember hadn't seen before. She bit her bottom lip and let out a long, low whistle that turned into a rambling melody. "You're awfully good at finding things, aren't you?" she asked softly. She pet the top of Ember's wide head and backed out of the kennel. "Hang in there, pup. I think I have an idea."

Ember listened to Jo's fading whistle, and turned around and lay down on the well-worn bed. She gnawed on her glove a little half-heartedly at first, and then with more enthusiasm. Along with the whistle, something in Jo's voice had changed again. The hopeful note . . . it was back.

04

Roxanne Valentine drank the last swig of coffee from her thermos, checked in the rearview mirror to make sure she didn't have any stray breakfast on her freckled face, and stepped out of her pickup truck. The sign on the glass door read ARROYO ANIMAL SERVICES, and she could hear dogs barking the moment she opened her car door. She was definitely in the right place. As she walked toward the entrance on her long legs, she tucked her auburn hair behind her ears. She hoped that the worker she spoke to was right about the Lab, that her early morning drive wasn't for nothing.

Jo Winston had called the day before to tell her about a dog she thought would be great for search and rescue . . . a dog out of options.

The bell over the door jangled as Roxanne stepped inside, and a young woman with a practical ponytail and a uniform that made her look like a park ranger looked up from behind the desk.

"You must be Roxanne!" she greeted her warmly, standing and offering a hand.

Roxanne nodded and returned the woman's easy smile. "You must be Jo." She extended her own hand. The pair shook, and Jo wasted no time leading her back to the kennels, where Ember was waiting. "She's a great dog, just a little . . . intense," Jo explained.

"And she's had how many families?" Roxanne asked. As the lead dog trainer at the Sterling Center, she knew that sometimes dogs who made terrible pets were terrific for search and rescue programs, the Sterling Center's specialty. But some dogs were difficult in any setting, and she couldn't just take Jo's word for it. If she brought this dog back to Sterling, it was a commitment—a commitment for the full life of the dog. The Sterling Center took the responsibility of bringing in a new dog seriously, because even if the dog wasn't able to complete the training and earn a certificate to be a search and rescue dog, they'd be responsible for finding it a new place to live. And it could be difficult to find an adult dog a home. Especially one with a checkered past.

"Three," Jo answered, wincing a little. She really hoped her hunch was right . . . that Ember could become a working dog.

Roxanne bit her lip. Dogs in shelters didn't often get fourth chances.

The barking grew louder as the two women walked down the row of kennels. Jo stopped in front of Ember's cage. She took down the clipboard hanging from the chain-link fencing and handed it to Roxanne to look over.

Roxanne scanned the pages, taking her time. The

dog was a good age for assessment—a little over a year. She was mostly Labrador retriever, which was a breed known for drive and energy and was usually well suited to tracking. "Good on paper," she murmured, more to herself than to Jo. She knew all too well that paper was the least of it. When assessing a rescue dog, Roxanne's number one resource was her gut.

"Let's get a look at you." She hung the clipboard back on the gate and observed the wagging dog on the other side of the fence. She was a warm, honey gold with slightly darker floppy ears, which matched the tip of her tail. Her dark-chocolate nose was the same shade as the "eyeliner" that rimmed her milk-chocolate eyes, which were bright and fixed on Roxanne.

"Hello," Roxanne said, and Ember's tail picked up speed, waving hello back. Then the dog turned quickly, grabbed something off the floor with her mouth, and presented it to Roxanne.

"What's this?" Roxanne squinted at the mangled chew toy. "Is that a . . . glove?"

Jo chuckled. She opened the gate and clipped a leash on Ember. "Yes. It's her favorite thing. She was rescued from a house fire when she was a puppy. She arrived here with that old thing and has taken it everywhere she's gone since."

"So she's loyal," Roxanne murmured. "To a glove. That's kind of perfect." Roxanne tugged the glove, tussling and playing with Ember, who wasn't the slightest bit shy or skittish even though they'd just met. Then she asked, "Can I have it, Ember?" She held out her hand and Ember gently deposited the slobbery glove in her open palm. "Thank you!" Roxanne gave Ember a quick pat. "Now, Jo, can you distract her for a minute? I want to check something else."

Jo looked confused but nodded. "Sure. Come on, Em!" She patted her thigh. Ember looked at Roxanne and her favorite glove, wondering if the game was over, then back at Jo, who gave her leash a tug. "Let's go find a treat!" Jo chirped. Ember followed a little reluctantly.

As soon as the dog's back was turned, Roxanne walked past the long row of dogs to the other end of the building and hid the glove on a high shelf out of the Lab's line of sight.

When she rejoined Jo and Ember, she was greeted again with wags, but this time Ember was looking for something. She snuffled Roxanne's hands, wondering where her glove had gone. Roxanne didn't say a word. She let Ember finish sniffing and took the leash from Jo. Ember pulled hard on the end, and Roxanne followed. The young dog was strong and clearly hadn't had good leash training. But that wasn't what Roxanne was watching for. Ember kept sniffing, pulling her along the row of barking dogs, some of whom were growling and challenging Ember aggressively. The yellow Lab stayed focused. When she reached the spot below the shelf where Roxanne had hidden the glove, she stopped. She sniffed the floor, then put her front feet up on the counter below the shelf and sniffed the air. She barked. Her glove was up there somewhere. She could smell it.

"Good job, Ember!" Roxanne took the glove down and returned it to the dog. She held the thumb, playing a little tug, and then let go so the Lab could swing the glove side to side in her mouth, giving it a good victory shake. "And I think you're right, Jo. Ember definitely has the stuff. The Sterling Center will take her."

Jo pumped her fist, a grin splitting her face. "I'll go start the paperwork!" she said. She spun around and left the kennels, whistling softly to herself.

Twenty minutes later, Roxanne led Ember out to the parking lot. They both turned when they heard the bell on the door jangle behind them.

"One more thing!" Jo jogged up and got down on

one knee. "Just wanted to say goodbye to this little firecracker," she said a bit wistfully. "I have a feeling you won't be back this time."

Ember cocked one of her ears and looked at Jo. The hopeful note was in her voice, but her smell was happy and sad. It was a new look, not the nervous face she'd worn before when Ember left with the old man and the other families.

Jo roughed up the fur on Ember's neck, and Ember landed a lick on her face. A goodbye.

"Okay, Ember!" Roxanne called. She patted the mat in the crate she kept inside her covered pickup truck. "Let's go." Roxanne placed Ember's glove in the crate and Ember jumped up without hesitation. She was immediately surrounded by the smells of other dogs, but none of them smelled sad or sick or scared.

"Good dog." Roxanne latched the crate and closed the back of the truck, talking calmly to Ember the whole time. When the truck engine rumbled to life, Ember turned once and lay down. She let the vibrations of the engine lull her to sleep and only woke when Roxanne was back and opening the tailgate and crate to let her out.

"We're here!" Roxanne said, smiling.

She clipped on Ember's leash but let the Lab take her time jumping down and exploring the spot where they'd stopped.

"Here" was a big place with lots of buildings and hills and dry grass and big trees. Here smelled of newly turned dirt and cooking and rain just a few days back. Here smelled strongly of dogs. Some fresh, some long gone. Here also smelled of people. Ember filled her nose again and again while Roxanne waited patiently, never yanking on her collar. Never choking her. Ember took one more whiff and then followed Roxanne into one of the large buildings.

She liked "here."

Here seemed nice.

She wagged.

Very nice.

05

"Well, who do we have here?" Frances Sterling stood up from behind the curved desk in the front office of the Sterling Center when Ember and Roxanne came in. She tucked a wisp of short white hair behind her ear and smiled at the new four-legged recruit, who was busy discovering everything she could about the building with her nose.

Though Frances had officially retired and turned the day-to-day operations over to her son Martin and daughter-in-law Georgia, the founder of the Sterling

Center still lived on the ranch and was always available to lend a hand when needed. Today Frances felt lucky to be filling in at the welcome center. Greeting new dogs was one of her favorite tasks.

"This is Ember," Roxanne said. She walked around the desk to give Frances a quick hug and dropped Ember's leash so the curious pup could explore every corner of the building.

Frances's blue eyes were bright as they followed the busy dog around the room. Dogs like Ember were the reason she'd started a training program more than a decade ago, after she'd retired the *first* time. Back then, though she was done with nursing, she knew she had something more to do. And looking at Sunshine, her dog at the time, she knew the golden retriever also had more to offer.

It hadn't taken Frances long to figure out how, together, they could really help people. In the face of disaster, dogs were not only great comfort, but had amazing search skills. They could do things no human could ever do, and most dogs only wanted a chance to help.

Eighteen years and many dogs and donations later, there was an entire wall in the welcome center covered with pictures and letters and awards—a testament to the many people (and dogs) who had been saved thanks to the Sterling family's efforts.

Frances glanced at the wall of pictures and then back at the new recruit. She patted her thigh, and Ember looked up from her sniffing and came over to say hello. Frances's own dog, Cocoa, stood up from her favorite spot under the front desk and tottered on creaky legs to get a whiff of the new dog.

Frances pet them both as they slowly circled each other, doing their doggy greetings. Ember wagged fast. Cocoa wagged more slowly.

At thirteen, Cocoa did everything more slowly. The chocolate Lab was retired, but she'd seen her share of adventures and was a hero many times over (with her own plaques on the wall to prove it). She'd earned every white hair on her muzzle—the soft white fur Frances's youngest grandchild liked to call her "whipped cream topping." Now, at this stage of life, Cocoa was content to be Frances's constant companion.

"Where'd you get this whippersnapper?" Frances asked, looking from Ember to Roxanne and back.

Ember was done sniffing the elderly woman and her dog, and had moved on to the spot by the printer, which had the distinct odor of cat. Also, someone had spilled coffee with cream next to the file cabinet. And next to *that* she thought she smelled mustard that had dripped out of a sandwich.

"I just picked her up from Arroyo Animal Services out in Big Fork," Roxanne reported. "She was surrendered yesterday . . . by her *third* family." Roxanne's green eyes narrowed as she watched Ember explore. She hoped she'd made the right call. Her dog instincts were good, but Frances's were better.

Frances raised her eyebrows and looked from the redheaded young woman to the golden-furred canine and back.

"Apparently she's quite a digger and a chewer. And she hates to be alone," Roxanne added.

"Perfect." Frances nodded approvingly. "She has work to do."

Roxanne smiled. As the founder of the Sterling Center, Frances understood dogs and had a lot of experience with all kinds and all breeds. She recognized that some dogs really *needed* to work.

"She's got plenty of energy!" Roxanne agreed. "Let's just hope I can get it focused." She stepped on the leash still dragging loosely and called Ember to the back door so she could get her settled in the canine pavilion, the building where they housed dogs in training.

Frances sat back down in the swivel chair and watched Roxanne and Ember through the window. She could tell Roxanne was feeling a little trepidation. It was hard not to want to save every dog—and not to believe every dog would do well at Sterling. She lifted Cocoa's wide head and looked into her milky eyes, smiling. "I think they're going to be just fine. Don't you?" she asked. Cocoa slow-wagged her agreement.

🐾 🐾 🐾

Outside on the ranch, Ember's nose was in overdrive and telling her to go in a hundred directions at once. Luckily, Roxanne was patient as the twosome made their way down the path that led from the front office to the canine pavilion, and she didn't seem to mind that Ember needed to stop and sniff along the way.

One side of the path was wooded—Ember could smell rotting leaves, squirrels, budding green plants, blue jays, oak trees . . . On the other side were more buildings, some with kitchens, some without, some with people, some without, and a wide, dry spot where many dogs had run.

"Here we go." Roxanne smiled down at Ember as they approached a building bigger than all the rest.

It smelled strongly of dogs, like the shelter Ember had just come from. She could smell kibble, treats, water, beds . . . There were more smells, too—lots that she didn't recognize, and one she definitely did: twelve-year-old boy!

Ember's last family had a twelve-year-old boy . . . Theo. He was her favorite because he didn't yell like Nancy. Sometimes he even joined in the backyard digging, and he almost always invited her up on the couch when nobody was looking. Theo also loved to tussle. And so did Ember!

The moment Roxanne opened the door to the pavilion, Ember nosed her way through and ran straight for the source of the smell.

Forrest Sterling had his earbuds in, listening to music as he sprayed the kennel runs with a powerful hose. At twelve, he had recently taken on a "real" job at the center and worked mornings and weekends cleaning kennels and feeding the dogs in training. He was nodding along to one of his favorite songs, mouthing the words while his black corkscrew curls flopped to the beat. He didn't hear the fifty-five pounds of furry enthusiasm barreling toward him until it was too late.

"Ember!" Roxanne shouted as the leash was yanked out of her hands.

Ember heard her name but did not stop. She ran headlong into Forrest, jumping and barking, and inviting him to play. Unbraced and on slick wet cement, Forrest toppled over.

"Whoa, whoa, whoa!" he shouted. He lost his grip on the hose that was locked on and shooting a powerful spray. It flailed in all directions. The startled boy hooted in surprise. Then he burst out laughing at the excited pup and the hose, which was acting like an angry snake as it flapped and spit and soaked his hair, his clothes, the floor, the dog . . . *everything.*

Ember caught the spray full in the face, but that only made the game more fun. She hopped over the thrashing hose and landed a wet lick on Forrest's cheek before bounding to his other side and barking another invitation to play.

Doubled over and trying to protect his face from being sprayed or licked, Forrest couldn't do a thing to stop the craziness.

Roxanne joined in the laughter as water blasted her legs and shoes. She was still chuckling as she calmly stepped on the hose, reached down, and turned off the nozzle.

"Well," she said, wiping tears from her eyes. "That was quite an introduction. Forrest, meet Ember. Ember, Forrest."

Forrest got to his knees and threw his arm over the wet dog's shoulder, grinning and revealing the small gap between his two front teeth. Half a second later, he pulled his arm back to shield his face while the Lab shook off the excess water.

"I suppose we should start with a bath since we're halfway there, anyway," Roxanne said. "Forrest, would you do the honors?"

Forrest shook his own head and scrambled up from the floor. "Sure," he agreed. Bathing the dogs wasn't something he usually did, but he was more than happy to lend a hand. Especially for this new bundle of wriggling enthusiasm.

Ember followed Forrest to the area they used for grooming with her tongue hanging out, panting happily. It wasn't dignified, but the hose game was the most fun she'd had in a long time, and it hadn't ended in yelling.

She tried to stay still while the gentle boy shampooed her and rinsed her in warm water. She only shook when the soap tickled too much or the dripping was too itchy. Then she had to let go, which sent suds flying and Forrest ducking for cover.

When she was thoroughly toweled, Forrest took Ember back to the place where they played hose and showed her to a kennel. "This will be your spot for a while," he explained. "While Roxanne gets you trained up."

"Here, give her this." Roxanne appeared behind them with Ember's glove, which she had just retrieved from her truck. "It might help her settle in. Nice job on the bath, by the way," she commended Forrest. "This one's not easy to contain." They both laughed at that and watched Ember take her chew glove over to the foam pad inside the enclosure.

Ember turned three times on the new bed and lay down. Roxanne and Forrest closed the gate. They stood a few steps away, watching Ember situate the glove between her front paws.

"You're pretty good with her," Roxanne told Forrest.

Forrest shot her a shy half smile.

"What's all this I hear about a new perro?" Pedro Sundal strode into the pavilion, surprising Roxanne and Forrest and widening their smiles. It was always good to see Pedro. He lived and worked on the ranch, too, and was in charge of training the handlers who the dogs would eventually live and work with. Together, he and Roxanne made up the lead training team at Sterling. The center was currently working on bringing in new trainers, as two had just departed.

Pedro and Roxanne liked to consult each other about everything. Roxanne clapped a hand on Pedro's shoulder. "Word travels fast!" she chuckled. "This is Ember. She just got here. She's a bit of a handful, but I think she's gonna make a crackerjack SAR dog."

Pedro ran his hand over his close-cut goatee and squatted down. He made a kissing sound with his lips. Ember came to the gate and licked his sun-weathered hand through the fencing.

Roxanne filled Pedro in on her morning's adventures, and he laughed at the story of the glove and the impromptu shower.

"Sounds like she'll be perfect for wilderness searches." Pedro nodded. "It's too bad we didn't get her a month or two ago. I've got a firefighter coming down from the mountains at the end of summer. They might have been a great match."

It wasn't hard to picture Ember combing the pine-covered hills of the Sierras.

"Maybe she'll be a fast learner," Forrest offered. "You never know."

Roxanne and Pedro smiled at the kid's optimism, but it could take anywhere from several months to two years to train a wilderness tracker. Pedro stood and Ember went back to her bed with her glove. She'd have to be super fast to be ready for a handler by the end of summer, and there was no rushing a dog through training.

"You never know," Roxanne said, not wanting to dampen Forrest's mood any more than his clothes. She put her hand on his wet shoulder so he would follow her out. She had something else she wanted to ask him.

Ember watched the trio disappear through the pavilion door—the boy with the curly hair, the woman with the speckled face, and the man with the hairy chin. She liked them. She wished they would stay. But hardly anyone ever did.

She chewed lightly on her glove, which released the smells held deep inside—smoke and leather and the scent of the man with the rumbling voice. The smells were familiar, and she loved that they were still there, after so much time. The glove and those smells were the only things that stayed the same in Ember's ever-changing world. Or at least so far. She hoped these new people would stick around a little longer.

06

Forrest slid into his chair at the large, square Sterling dining table, his blue eyes darting around excitedly. He had news he could not wait to share! He lifted his fork and tapped it absently on the table, impatiently waiting for the rest of the family to arrive. His older sister, Shelby, sauntered into the room, flung her pink-streaked hair behind one shoulder, and slid into her seat. She pursed her lips, shooting Forrest her usual look of disapproval. Forrest ignored her, set his fork on his napkin, and gnawed his thumbnail. Shelby was fourteen and thought she had authority over the rest of her siblings. She was always telling him to sit still or stop fidgeting . . . or anything else she could think of.

"Don't bite your nails." She swatted at Forrest's hand. Forrest dodged.

"Don't tell me what to do," he shot back breezily. Aside from her lack of dimples and lighter, pink-streaked hair, which Forrest secretly thought was cool, Shelby looked just like their mom. She had the same light brown skin, same dark almond-shaped eyes, same straight nose—but that didn't mean she could act like her!

Shelby tried to fix her brother with a stare.

Forrest only shrugged. Usually his big sister's nagging bugged him. Tonight it had no effect. He was too excited.

Shelby didn't snap back but kept her eyes fixed on her brother—something was up.

Juniper arrived next and took her spot next to Shelby, her hazel eyes locking on the basket of corn bread. She was hungry and ready to pounce, but knew better than to help herself before everyone was seated.

Morgan, who was ten and closest to Forrest in age and disposition, brought the butter dish in from the kitchen. She took a seat beside her brother and bent to look underneath the table for her grandmother's dog. Their grandmother Frances was just taking her seat, too. She lived in her own small cottage but frequently joined them for meals and always brought Cocoa, the only "pet" dog living on the ranch. Morgan puckered her lips and threw Cocoa a kiss when she spotted her, not under the table but lying on the cool wood floor with her back against the sideboard.

Finally the children's parents, Georgia and Martin, emerged from the kitchen, carrying a large pot of chili and a big green salad. They placed their offerings in the center of the table before settling themselves and giving the signal to dig in.

All around the table, Sterlings began serving up. Juniper dove on the corn bread, placing two pieces in a small tower on her plate . . . she was the youngest and smallest, but ate more than anyone. She got a withering look from Shelby, but before Shelby could scold her, an obviously excited Forrest blurted the news he'd been dying to share. "We've got a new dog and Roxanne wants me to be the training assistant!"

Everyone at the table stopped what they were doing and looked at Forrest. Everyone understood that what Forrest had just announced was news and a big deal.

"Hold on now." Georgia's arm, which had been shaking hot sauce on her chili, froze in midair. "I think this is a *conversation* we need to have, not an *announcement*," she said. Her words were stern but her dark eyes were gentle.

Forrest looked at his mom and clamped his mouth shut. Georgia was in charge of pretty much everything and was as fierce as she was loving. She handled the daily operations at the Sterling Center, officially since Frances had stepped down, and mostly before that, too. She took care of the business side of things for the nonprofit center, managing money and people. She also handled any press or publicity, always with a calm and steady hand, always looking for solutions that would be best for everyone involved. Georgia was also the chief dreamer and had big plans for what the center could and should become. What Martin's mother had started had become an incredible rescue resource and could be so much more! But before any of her Sterling Center responsibilities, Georgia was Juniper, Morgan, Shelby, and Forrest's mom—a job she did not take lightly.

"We need to talk about what this means with school and the chores you already have," Georgia said. She handed the hot sauce to Morgan, who shared her love of spicy food, and smoothed her long curly hair away from her face—a habit that never accomplished anything since it always sprang back. Georgia looked meaningfully at her husband, her brown eyes locking with his blue.

Martin knew exactly what Georgia's look meant. It said "we need to handle this carefully."

"You've got a lot on your plate, Forrest," Martin said, backing up his wife. Most of the time, the two of them were on the same page when it came to parenting, but he had a lighter touch than she did and was not as prone to worrying about the ways things might go wrong.

Besides dad duties, Martin was in charge of maintenance at Sterling—and there was a lot of it with so many buildings and new things happening all the time. He was the construction manager for all additions and the on-call fix-it guy—which applied to people as well as buildings and vehicles.

"Summer is almost here," Forrest said, and then zipped his lips. In this case, saying less was better.

"Forrest has been doing well keeping up with the dog care and schoolwork," Martin said. "Once school is out . . ." He raised an eyebrow and ran a hand over his thinning blond hair.

Forrest twitched in his seat. He gulped and looked at his hands in his lap. When he glanced up, his grandma was looking right at him with her slightly sly smile, watching it all play out. She winked. Forrest tried to wink back.

Frances understood how much it meant to the boy to become a training assistant . . . the two of them had more in common than their twinkly blue eyes.

And Frances wasn't the only one who knew what a big deal it would be if Forrest got to work with Roxanne and the new dog. Morgan dreamed of that day! She'd been around the search and rescue dogs, trainers, and handlers since she was born. She had read every book she could get her hands on, from the Sterling Center and local libraries. If there was such a thing as a child expert in SAR dogs, Morgan was sure she was it. Which is why she knew that if Forrest worked with the new dog, she wouldn't. It was important that every dog have one dedicated trainer and one dedicated, regular assistant. It was important so the dogs wouldn't get confused and so that they could successfully bond with the handler they'd be matched with later on for work in the field.

"So can I do it?" Forrest asked, interrupting the silent conversation his parents were having with their eyebrows. "Roxanne is going to start with obedience. Ember's kind of hyper and easily distracted."

"Kind of!" Shelby's voice dripped sarcasm. She'd seen Roxanne walking the dog to the pavilion and had steered clear. They got all kinds of dogs at Sterling, but Ember was one of the least focused she'd ever seen, constantly pulling in different directions after this squirrel or that smell, or this moving leaf, or . . .

Forrest shot Shelby a look. Shelby pretended not to notice and served herself a heap of salad.

"By the time Rox is done with obedience, school will be out!" Forrest finished. "So . . ."

Georgia and Martin both nodded yes at the same time, while Frances smiled into her napkin.

"Yesss!" Forrest celebrated by snatching the basket of corn bread from Juniper, who was taking her third. "Save some for the rest of us," he chided.

Nobody noticed that Morgan was slumping—she'd gone suddenly boneless with the news—nobody but Cocoa, who appeared by her leg and rested her wide head in her lap to soothe her disappointment. Morgan pet the old pooch under the table, not caring that doing so was forbidden.

"This is going to be great," Forrest said loudly, oblivious that he had just snagged Morgan's dream job.

Morgan scratched Cocoa's ear and searched for a bright side. If Forrest was busy working as a training assistant, maybe she would be able to help with his canine care chores and cleaning. That would at least get her some more time with the dogs, which was the most important thing to her, anyway.

Always.

07

"I hate that we're stuck in here while Forrest is out there," Morgan grumbled from the observation trailer on the edge of the training grounds. She tugged on one of her short twists in frustration. Given her brother's promotion three weeks ago, the fact that she was in here with her two sisters doing two things she didn't like—watching and waiting—was making her extra grumpy.

Shelby rolled her eyes and threw a hand on her skinny-jeaned hip—her know-it-all, older-sister stance.

Not that Shelby *did* know it all . . . especially about the dogs.

"Come on, Morgan. You know only one of us gets to be out there with Roxanne." Shelby wasn't in the best mood, either. Watching a training session at nine thirty on a Saturday morning was not her first choice, but her plans to hang out with her best friend, Alice, fell through at the last minute, and since she was already up . . . Plus she kind of wanted to see Ember's first real crack at finding a victim— Forrest. So far Ember had watched Forrest run away and then followed, "finding" him. But today he was going to disappear without Ember watching. Today the new dog would have to use her nose to find him. It was a big step.

"You're too young to work with the dogs, anyway," Shelby added, watching Morgan's face screw up into a scowl. She didn't really mean to take her annoyance out on her sister, especially because she knew how Morgan felt about being left out of dog training.

Before she started high school, she'd felt the same way. Now that she was finished with her freshman year, though, she didn't care as much about dogs and dog training as she used to. There were too many other things to do. The local high school was four times the size of her middle school, the homework was *way* harder, and she'd made a lot of new friends she didn't want to lose track of over the summer . . . especially a certain cute boy named Ryan, who had arrived at the school in the spring of last year and only just started talking to her in biology class.

"Don't you have some friends to go hang out with or something?" Morgan shot back. It wasn't like her to be mean, but sometimes Shelby brought out the worst in her. She bit her lower lip guiltily and pressed her nose to the glass.

Outside, Roxanne was ready with Ember's red-and-white search and rescue vest. Buckling on the vest was the very first part of a training session. Not only was it essential for the dog to be easily identified in the field, the dog needed to get used to the vest so that it felt comfortable and natural and did not distract them. During rescues the vest might be worn for hours on end—sometimes even days. Strapping on the vest also sent a clear message to the dog that it was time to get to work, or in this case time to start training. Unfortunately, that message wasn't clear to Ember. At least not yet. She was wagging and jumping up on Roxanne, who couldn't get her to stay still long enough to fasten the buckles.

"Dogs are such dorks!" Juniper sniffed, gazing out the trailer window and squeezing the cat in her arms more tightly. "Not dignified like you, Twiggy." Twig let out a sharp meow and wriggled weakly in resistance in spite of the compliment. He was used to being toted around by Juniper, but that didn't mean he always liked it.

"Meeeooowwwww," the big orange tabby protested.

"I agree, Twiggy," Juniper replied, as if Twig had spoken perfect English. "You're much smarter . . ."

She leaned forward and cooed in his ear. "You could absolutely do a better job."

Shelby watched Juniper flip the hair their mom kept braided in two long black plaits onto her back and smirked at the littlest Sterling. Leave it to Juniper to think she could train a cat for rescue! Being the youngest, she was constantly on the lookout for something that would make her stand out from her dog-obsessed family.

Outside, Roxanne was oblivious to the sisters in the trailer. She was all focus, and Ember was all play. "Ember, stay!" the trainer said firmly. She didn't raise her voice—it never helped. Besides, Roxanne had already seen progress in the yellow Lab mix, and she knew from experience that training was incremental and *not* always linear. Sometimes you made a little progress. Sometimes you slipped back. Sometimes you went sideways . . . the path was different for every dog. The most important thing was for the humans to be consistent. To help the dog anticipate. To help the dog trust both their handlers and their own instincts.

Ember reminded Roxanne of Cascade, one of the many dogs her family had when she was a child. Like Ember, Cade had been feisty and energetic. And when it came to their pets, the Valentine family tended to be big on love and not so big on training . . . they never did get Cade to sit and stay. The messages were always mixed.

Roxanne sighed at the memory of her energetic and sometimes crazy-making dog and gazed down at young Ember. She wanted to get the Lab focused on tracking Forrest's scent, but at the moment, Ember was only focused on licking Roxanne's freckled cheek.

Roxanne tried not to laugh as she reminded Ember to sit. Dogs like Ember and Cade were the reason she became a trainer. She'd always adored dogs and their incredible, unbridled spirit. But when she was growing up, the unchecked chaos spirited dogs created in her house—which was already chaotic because there were five kids—was enough to drive anyone a little bonkers. Especially the dogs themselves. She'd discovered that, with very rare exceptions, dogs loved to be trained. It helped them to thrive, and to relax.

"Stay," Roxanne repeated calmly but firmly. Ember stilled—a result of the weeks they'd been working. "Good stay," Roxanne praised her, bending down to strap and buckle the vest at last. With the vest secured, she double-checked that the long lead coiled around her arm wasn't tangled. She was standing next to a marked-off "scent pad"—a spot on the grass where Forrest had wiped his feet several times in order to deposit his particular smell. After just a few foot swipes, even with shoes on, the spot on the grass was super-loaded smell-wise, even for an untrained dog like Ember.

Ember's nose was her superpower. Like any dog, she was capable of smelling one part per trillion, or one drop from an eyedropper deposited somewhere in a city the size of Philadelphia. The trick, Roxanne knew, was teaching a dog to locate that smell, to isolate it from all the other smells in the wider world.

In their first weeks of training, they had succeeded with obedience, and then beginner runaway, or the very early "find" game. Over and over, Forrest had gotten Ember's attention, gotten her to follow him, and then ducked out of view. The minute he disappeared, Roxanne had told Ember to "find." She'd succeeded and was ready to move on.

After leaving his smell on the scent pad, Forrest had strategically hidden about 150 feet away behind the bleachers on the edge of the training ground. He was the "victim"—the person Ember had to search for. Then, before bringing Ember out, Roxanne had placed a few treats between the scent pad and Forrest, to encourage Ember to move in the right direction. Roxanne didn't make things too complicated—initial search sessions were kept simple so that a dog had a better chance at success.

"Here." Roxanne indicated the scent pad and waited for Ember to get a good whiff.

Ember stuck her nose into the short blades of grass and snuffled up the scent. More than the odor left by the shoes, she could smell the tiny skin particles that humans were constantly shedding. When she had a snout full, she looked up at Roxanne.

"Find," Roxanne instructed.

Ember let out an excited bark in response.

"Find," Roxanne repeated the command.

This time Ember sat down and cocked her head to one side, her eyes trained on Roxanne. She could smell Forrest, but she didn't see him anywhere.

"Find," Roxanne said a third time.

All at once, Ember was back on her feet. She had an idea. She was pretty sure she knew what Roxanne wanted her to do, and it wasn't sitting or staying! She turned away from Roxanne and moved toward the boy smell. Before getting too far, she found a treat and gobbled it down. A few strides later, she found another. She ate that, too, and licked her lips.

"Good job, Ember," Roxanne called. "Find!" she repeated.

Roxanne's voice was encouraging, and Ember wagged. She liked this new game! She liked treats!

"She's doing it!" Morgan cheered from the trailer and bounced on the soles of her feet. Her nose left a smear on the glass when she stepped back to clap her hands together. Beside her, Twig struggled in Juniper's arms . . . he didn't like the trailer. It smelled strongly of dog, and Twig did not like dogs. Luckily for the canines that were everywhere on the ranch, he was able to tolerate them. But new, untrained dogs were the worst.

"She looks good in her vest," Shelby said. She was enjoying this more than she thought she would. "The red brings out the gold in her fur."

"Yeah," Morgan agreed as the three girls watched the dog's progress. "And look, she's closing in on Forrest."

"Find!" Roxanne called once more, her voice strong and steady.

Ember turned back to her trainer. There were no more treats, and the smell of boy was both in front of her and behind her, which was confusing. She hesitated for just a second. Then she took off at a run, barreling toward Roxanne at full speed.

"Ember, no!"

It was too late. The dog ran several circles around Roxanne, tying her long legs up in the lead like a rodeo calf and sending her toppling to the ground. Ember sniffed her pocket for more treats, her nose quivering excitedly. She *really* liked to find.

"No, Ember." Roxanne suppressed a laugh but could not hide her smile as she scrambled to her feet and untangled herself. It was true that Ember found the treats Roxanne had left along the trail, and then she'd found the place that they had come from, but that wasn't what she was supposed to be searching for!

"Come on out, Forrest," Roxanne called. "We'll have to try again." She wondered if they should wait until the next day to try again. There was no written rule—every dog was different. But sometimes it was best to take an overnight break after a failed exercise so the dog could start clean. Roxanne had a hunch this might be the best way to go with Ember so that she didn't reinforce searching for treats!

Just a moment later, Forrest appeared from behind the bleachers, and Ember took off at another dead run, yanking Roxanne's arm when she reached the end of her lead. Roxanne held her ground . . . she was accustomed to this. Ember stopped and stood still. She let out a bark and wagged so hard her whole back end swung back and forth. Twelve-year-old boy was one of her favorite smells, and the real boy was so much better than the boy-scented grass patch.

Forrest knew he couldn't give Ember attention as he passed—she hadn't completed her task, so he couldn't reward her with affection. It wasn't meant as punishment so much as a natural consequence. Still, it was hard to ignore the barking, wagging pup.

Ember trotted along behind Forrest, a little bewildered that he hadn't stopped for a tussle or pet. By the time they got to Roxanne, Forrest's sisters had emerged from the observation trailer and had their dark heads all dipped together in a huddle near the trainer.

Twig was struggling in Juniper's arms even more mightily than before, which Ember took as an invitation. She lunged playfully, eager to greet the girls and get a good whiff of cat.

"Reeooowwww!" Twig yowled. He dug his claws into Juniper's arm, making the girl howl right along with him. Then he gave a final, determined squirm and jumped to the ground, back arched and hissing.

Ember barked excitedly, unaware of the cat's disdain. She'd never been this close to a cat before. Curious, she wiggled closer to the now-sidestepping Twig.

Twig halted and reached out an angry claw, swiping the pup's face before bolting away. Thinking fast, Roxanne grabbed Ember's collar before she could give chase.

"Twig!" Juniper ran after the fleeing feline, braids flying behind her. She didn't like it when her favorite animal got farther than an arm's length away.

Ember sat down on her haunches, stunned.

Ever steady, Roxanne drew a deep breath and let it out in a heavy but calm sigh. That sealed it. They would definitely stop training for the day. Too many distractions. Too much chaos. It would be confusing for Ember to try again now. They would have to start scent training again tomorrow, from the beginning.

Disappointment about the session hung over everyone like a dark cloud . . . even Shelby looked bummed. The only creature without a frown or furrowed brow had four legs and a golden coat. She spun in a circle, fully recovered from the cat attack, and wagged at the cluster of humans. This was the best home she'd been in so far, paws down, and to show them, she lowered her front half in a puppy play bow and wondered what game came next.

08

Forrest flopped onto his back and stretched from head to toe. He loved not having to wake up to an alarm . . . summer vacation was the best! The days were long and warm, and best of all school and home-work were blissfully absent. Rolling onto his side, he glanced at the clock and—uh-oh! He shoved his covers aside and leaped from the bed. He'd slept right through the most carefree moment of his day. He'd have to move fast to get his dog chores done before Ember's morning training session. Maybe summer wasn't so hassle-free after all!

Being a training assistant had come with a lot of new responsibility, and took more time than he'd imagined . . . especially because he was still doing all of his other jobs, namely dog care. Not that Forrest was complaining. Even though his plate was extra full, he loved working with Ember and Roxanne.

Just thinking about Ember made Forrest smile. He grabbed a not-too-dirty shirt off the floor and yanked it over his head. He did not want to disappoint Rox or Ember by being late. After a few false starts and Roxanne rodeo wrap-ups, Ember was starting to understand what she was supposed to do when she got a "find" command. Some days she still had a hard time containing her excitement, but those tricky days and training sessions were fewer and farther between. So far this week, Ember had found him three times, and he was now hiding three-hundred-plus yards away and in different places on the ranch—near the shade shelter, next to the agility course, even out past the rubble pile. Progress!

After Ember mastered "finds" without seeing Forrest leave, they'd moved on to "alerts." During this phase, Roxanne helped Ember learn how to "alert" her that she had found Forrest. This was crazy important, because finding a victim in a real-life rescue wouldn't do any good if the dog didn't communicate the find to the handler! Different dogs were naturally disposed to different kinds of alerts, and it quickly became clear that Ember's preferred alert was staying with Forrest and barking until Roxanne got the message. They'd also started using "scent articles"—pieces of clothing that smelled like Forrest. This week they were working on weaning her off the scent pad and making Forrest trickier to find.

Forrest zipped his jeans and walked by the mirror in his room without even checking it. He knew that if his mom saw him she would stop him to detangle his hair with her fingers, re-coil each curl neatly, and plead with him to let her put in a little coconut oil to keep it shiny. But he didn't have a minute to waste trying to make his curls behave. The last thing he wanted was to let something fall off his extra-full plate. Miraculously, the bathroom was sister (and especially Juniper)–free. You'd think his eight-year-old sister was a teenager the way she hogged the bathroom, and he shuddered to think about what was going to happen when she actually turned thirteen!

In the kitchen, Forrest made a quick piece of toast and slathered it with peanut butter before dashing to the canine pavilion. Still chewing, he threw open the door and realized that he wasn't the first to arrive . . . Morgan was there humming to herself and filling dog bowls with kibble.

Forrest's mood soured in an instant. Feeding was *his* job. The pavilion housed five dogs right now, and each one had specific dietary needs. If Morgan messed this up . . .

"Hey, what are you doing?" he growled. He stepped between her and the labeled containers of dog food.

"You need to read the chart. They don't all get the same food, you know . . ."

He trailed off as it dawned on him that Morgan was doing exactly that. Ember, Bucko, and the three other dogs all had the right kibble in what looked like the right amounts in their bowls. And glancing at the kennels, he saw that they already had fresh water and, even more impressive, clean cages.

"Never mind. I mean, um, thanks," Forrest mumbled sheepishly.

"No problem," Morgan replied, eyeing him from behind her twists, which stopped at her raised brows. "I figured with everything you've been doing around here lately you could use a little help."

Forrest's jaw hung a little loose because he didn't know what to say. She was right, and he was grateful—he really was. But he was also afraid. If Roxanne or his parents found out that he'd overslept and Morgan had to cover for him, they might take away his new training responsibilities. Skipping out on, or even *accidentally* missing chores was not okay on the ranch. The dogs relied on the humans for care, and the dogs came first. That was rule number one.

Forrest was trying to put these jumbled thoughts into words when Twig interrupted with a plaintive meow. He turned and spotted the orange cat sitting atop a cabinet, twitching his tail and gazing intently at Ember. "Mrrrrroooowwwrr," the tabby complained again, more loudly this time. It was weird to see Twig in the pavilion. He generally avoided the doggiest spots on the ranch, but ever since Twig and Ember encountered each other on the training ground and Twig swiped Ember's snout, the cat had been lurking around the dogs, especially Ember. Forrest hadn't ever seen Twig act like this before, and was a little annoyed because he could tell that the cat was distracting Ember during training. Juniper would disagree loudly, but Forrest suspected that Twig was doing it on purpose!

"Morning, everybody," Roxanne called as she came

through the door. Ember's training log was tucked securely under her arm . . . she carried it almost everywhere she went these days. Every dog had one—a dedicated logbook filled with detailed notes on each and every training session, general comments about a dog's progress, disposition, ideas for the dog's future, etc. By the time a dog left Sterling, every page in its log would be filled with information. She had just given Pedro a glimpse of Ember's progress. She was doing so well they were both feeling hopeful that she might be ready to be introduced to the handlers coming soon—the one looking for a wilderness tracker in particular!

Roxanne completed her nearly instantaneous check of the pavilion and nodded approvingly. "Looks like you were up early this morning, Forrest," she said. "Excellent work."

Morgan raised her brows in her brother's direction, making her big brown eyes even bigger, as if to say, "Well?" But Forrest only nodded sheepishly, not giving Morgan an ounce of credit for what was entirely her work.

In a flash, Morgan's expression shifted into a storm cloud of frustration. She turned away from Forrest and reached up to pull the yowling tabby cat off his perch. "I agree, Twig," she said. "Something in here stinks."

Twig didn't protest about being scooped up. Unlike Juniper, Morgan never squeezed too hard.

Forrest swallowed a lump of guilt. He was glad he couldn't see his sister's face as the twosome made their way to the door. He knew he'd just blown it with her, but Roxanne took dog care as seriously as she took training, and if he'd told the truth, she might have been angry with him or—almost worse—disappointed. He couldn't risk losing his promotion. No way. Even Morgan should under-stand that.

"Reeeooowwww," Twig yowled one last time. Forrest turned and saw that the cat was looking over

Morgan's shoulder. His green eyes were still locked on Ember, who stood beside Roxanne on a short lead.

"You ready, Forrest?" Roxanne asked. She obviously was, and so was Ember. The dog's vest was on, and she was looking at Rox expectantly, ready to get to work.

"Yes!" Forrest replied a little loudly. "Yes, I'm ready."

Outside, Forrest veered away from Roxanne and Ember and wiped his feet several times on a patch of dirt next to the obstacle course . . . a new scent pad. Ember was transitioning to scent articles more and more, but Roxanne had asked him to make one. With that accomplished, he set off to hide out by the woodpile. It was farther than he'd ever hidden before, and Ember would have to pass through training grounds and go behind the house in order to find him, with no treats on the way! It was what Roxanne called "leveling-up" day—a day when they upped the challenge for a dog in training.

Forrest jogged past the rubble pile, where dogs practiced searching on unstable ground like they might encounter after explosions or earthquakes. Forrest had always known that the Sterling Center had all kinds of structures and scenarios set up on the sprawling ranch to train its dogs. Still, when he saw them in person, he was always newly impressed at the lengths his family would go to make the training areas real. Dropping down beside a stand of trees, Forrest settled in for the hardest part of being a training assistant . . . the wait.

Back beside the scent pad, Roxanne waited for Ember to get still before giving the command. "Find!" she called, and Ember wagged. She knew exactly what this meant! She snuffed her way over to the spot in the dirt where Forrest had wiped his feet. She blew out with her breath, sending scent particles swirling up and into her nose. She didn't really need to. She knew what she was looking for.

"Find," Roxanne said again.

Ember moved quickly. Her feet were sure, and the scent trail was clear. She trotted along, following almost precisely the path that Forrest had taken. The trail was fresh—he'd just walked it a few minutes ago—which made the task fairly easy for her. She was good at this game.

"Good, Ember. Find!" Roxanne panted, a little out of breath from racing after the golden Lab. Four legs were definitely faster than two!

Ember rounded the rubble pile and made a beeline for the cluster of trees where Forrest was hidden. She jumped all over him, greeting her twelve-year-old boy with sloppy kisses. Forrest was supposed to ignore the greeting, and did, though this was the second-hardest thing about being a training assistant!

"Speak, Ember." He corrected her firmly so she would remember to do a proper alert. She was supposed to stand at attention and bark when she found her victim, not lick them to death.

Taking a step back, Ember looked at Forrest with

her big brown eyes, sat down, and began barking loudly—a perfect alert! She really did know what to do . . . sometimes she just forgot!

"Good job, Ember," Roxanne said, appearing between the trees. She offered her a liver treat, which Ember gratefully accepted. "And nice correction, Forrest. She really needs to complete the search with that final communication. If she doesn't alert her handler to let them know where she and the victim are, all her hard work could be of no use."

Ember sat down on her haunches, watching Roxanne closely. With a laugh, Roxanne realized what she was waiting for . . . her favorite treat of all. She pulled the tattered glove out of her satchel and handed it to Forrest, and the two began a rambunctious game of glove tug. Ember loved to work and to train, but she didn't love anything as much as that glove!

09

"Stop being so wiggly, Twiggy!" Juniper scolded the squirming cat in a whisper. Her arms were tired. She had been holding Twig for a loooong time, and they had to stay still because they were on a stakeout. About thirty yards away, out in the field, Roxanne was having a general training session with Ember. The tree Juniper and Twig were hiding behind was a tall pine, but it wasn't very wide, making it tricky for the wiry girl to remain completely out of sight and watch at the same time.

Juniper stood up straighter and peeked around the edge.

"Sit, Ember," Roxanne instructed. Ember sat obediently at Roxanne's feet, never taking her gaze off her trainer. "Stay." Roxanne turned and walked away from Ember . . . toward the tree!

"Reeeooowww!" Twig yowled at the approaching person.

"Shhh, Twiggy," Juniper corrected. "We don't want her to hear us!"

Fortunately, Roxanne was focused on Ember and didn't react to the yowling. When she was about halfway between Ember and the tree, she stopped and turned back to the dog. Ember, who was no longer on a lead for training sessions, hadn't moved an inch.

"Ember, come!" Roxanne called. Ember rose onto her four paws and trotted over to her. "Excellent stay and come!" Roxanne praised, giving her a treat and ruffling her ears.

"Like that's impressive." Juniper rolled her eyes and scratched Twig under his chin distractedly. "That dog is still pretty squirrelly if you ask me." Juniper didn't really care about Ember's progress. She was watching because she had a serious plan to start search and rescue training with Twig. Soon. And despite the fact that Roxanne was devoted to the wrong species, there was no denying her skill as a trainer. She could teach a dog to do almost anything . . . even a silly one like Ember.

"Okay, Ember," Roxanne said. "Review time!" She gave the command. "Find!"

Juniper was half relieved that she and Twig would be able to move from their hiding spot, and half grumpy that she had to walk somewhere else. Her legs were as tired as her arms! To make matters worse, she had to hold Twig extra tight because as soon as Ember was really on the move, the cat seemed to think he had to be on the go, too.

"Hold still!" Juniper whispered hoarsely as she

crept along behind Roxanne . . . who was behind Ember . . . who was looking for Forrest.

"Reow!" Twig objected. Juniper swung her arms around to carry him on her right side, almost dropping him in the process. "REEEEOOOWWW!" Twig was suddenly all claws and twitching tail. Juniper had to stop walking for several minutes to wrangle him, and by the time she caught up to Roxanne, Ember had already found Forrest. She barked the alert and the training session was over.

Juniper approached the threesome as calmly and as casually as she could—she had no desire to let them know she'd been watching their work. She wanted it to seem like a coincidence, like she was just out strolling with a heavy cat.

"Way to go, Ember!" Forrest crowed as he and Roxanne exchanged a high five.

Juniper tried not to scoff. "What's all the celebrating about?" she asked. Seriously. How hard could it be to sniff out a twelve-year-old boy? *She* could do that, and her nose was human! As the bathroom queen of the household, she saw all that went on in the tub and tile kingdom, and knew for a fact that Forrest only showered when their mom made him.

"Ember's almost ready to start working with a handler!" Forrest explained, wiping his sweaty brow on his T-shirt, which, Juniper noted, was filthy. "She's really making progress."

At the mention of Ember's name, Twig squirmed the squirm of a lifetime, finally breaking free from Juniper's arms. He leaped to the ground and landed gracefully on all fours in a puff of dust. His back semi-arched, he eyed the Lab warily, moving in a steady arc around the cluster of dog and humans. Ember was still sitting on her haunches but kept her eyes glued on the cat watching her every move. Juniper reached out to snatch Twig back up, but the cat hopped away from her and toward Ember, who responded by dropping into a full play bow.

Then, before anyone knew what was happening,

Ember let out an excited bark and bounded toward Twig.

"Ember, no," Roxanne scolded firmly. The Lab was wearing her vest and was still technically "working."

"Reow!" the cat taunted. Half a second later, Twig sprinted away, which gave Ember, being a dog, no choice but to give chase. Roxanne, Forrest, and Juniper watched as the cat hightailed it across the training grounds and ducked under a low fence.

"Ember!" Roxanne attempted to recall the dog, but Ember kept right on running.

"Rawr, rawr, rawr!" Her booming bark echoed as she bounded after the cat and sped across the lot, past the unstable earthquake rubble, and toward the area where they were getting ready to bring in the shell of a bus and some cars to re-create a highway disaster scene.

"Twwwiiiiiggg!" Juniper yelled as loud as she could. She felt almost embarrassed. Only a dog could get her sweet kitty to behave in such a terrible manner!

"Ember!" Roxanne called, but without much oomph. Ember and Twig were long gone. She dropped her head and started walking slowly in the direction the animals had disappeared.

"Ugh," Forrest mumbled. "That can't be good."

Roxanne nodded grimly. "It's strange we haven't seen this before. Prey drive is essential in a tracker. We need dogs to go after a target, but if they get distracted by every squirrel or cat or rodent they meet . . ."

Forrest bit his lower lip. It was one thing for the family dog to chase a cat, and something entirely different for a SAR dog to be sidetracked in the field where lives were at stake.

Roxanne let out her breath in one big huff. Their golden-furred Labrador was obviously not as close to working with a handler as they'd hoped.

10

"Here, kitty, kitty!" Juniper stood at the back door and shook the dry cat food container. She'd been there for half an hour, and her shoulders slumped as she stared into the yard. "Twiiig," she called. She wanted to see him walk aloofly up the back steps and rub against her leg. She wanted to see the impatient look he always had when he was waiting for his breakfast. But Twig was not there . . . for the second day in a row. Juniper was sure it was all Ember's fault. "Stupid dog," she muttered under her breath—practically a curse for a Sterling.

After the big chase with the rambunctious Lab, Twig had stayed away from the house all day. When he finally came in after dinner, his fur was matted and full of burrs. Juniper spent hours pulling them out one by one, while Twig complied by sitting still and complaining loudly. For several days after that, Twig had acted normal—aloof as ever, waiting expectantly for breakfast and dinner, letting Juniper tote him around, and sleeping on his special pillow next to hers all night long. Perfectly normal.

Until this morning. Juniper blinked back worried tears as she set the food on the counter and stepped into the slip-on shoes her mom kept by the back door. She stomped down the stairs and began to search the yard for signs of her precious kitty.

It *really* wasn't like him to miss a meal. In fact, Juniper couldn't remember that *ever* happening before—not even after he had to have a tooth pulled!

Juniper finished her tour of the yard and stomped back up the stairs and into the kitchen. Her dad was sipping coffee and gave her one of his "concerned" looks.

"Don't worry, June Bug." He placed a hand on her head, and Juniper ducked away like a cat being pet backward. If she knew how to hiss, she probably would have done that, too.

Martin didn't take Juniper's reaction personally. As the father of four, he knew better. And he knew Juniper. "Twig is a smart cat," he said reassuringly. "He'll be back."

"Twig's gone?" Forrest asked as he raced into the kitchen and started opening cupboards and gathering food. He was behind, as usual. No matter how hard he tried to wake up on time, he never did. And this far into training he had to "lose" himself *really* far away, which took extra time.

"Yes, Twig is gone," Morgan confirmed from her seat at the table. She was reading a new book on wilderness rescues over a bowl of cereal and didn't bother to look up. Normally she would have been out in the pavilion helping with the dogs by now, but why should she if Forrest wasn't going to give her any credit?

"It looks like it . . . at least for the moment," Martin said soberly.

"Good!" Forrest replied. "I swear that cat is trying to sabotage Ember. He's always slinking around when we're trying to get her focused, and he totally baited her last week. Roxanne almost didn't want to start working on advanced areas! She said Ember might be too easily distracted, but Twig was *asking* to be chased."

Within two seconds, Juniper was in the middle of the kitchen, hands firmly planted on her hips. "Don't go blaming Twig for your dog's stupid behavior," she snapped. "It's not his fault she's out of control."

Martin looked from Juniper to Forrest and back to Juniper. He shot a glance in Morgan's direction—hoping for a little rational backup—but his middle daughter was glued to her book. Martin cleared his throat. "Arguing about the animals is not going to make things better," he said with a serious face. Then he brightened a bit. "How about you and me take a walk, June Bug? Grab the food and we can search the property for your Twig."

Juniper let out a little huff of breath. "Fine," she said. "But I don't want to go anywhere near the dogs—especially not that wild one Forrest is in looooove with." She glared at Forrest, who just barely managed not to stick his tongue out at his littlest sister.

"Okay by me," Martin agreed. "No dogs." He steered his youngest out of the kitchen, shooting Forrest and Morgan a "wish us luck" look. Glancing up from her book at last, Morgan smiled and watched them go. She really had to give Juniper credit for her devotion to Twig—she loved that cat more than anything. Almost as much as Morgan loved dogs.

Forrest peeked at the large kitchen clock and let out a quiet groan. It was nearly nine, and he still hadn't eaten or started his dog chores.

Morgan closed her book and got up from the table. Eyeing her brother, she carried her cereal bowl to the sink and sighed. It was no use. She was really only torturing herself.

"You want help? Before Roxanne gets here?" she asked with a hand on her hip and a single eyebrow raised—a trick she had learned from their mom. She wasn't doing this for Forrest, she told herself. She was doing it for the dogs.

"Would you mind?" Forrest asked with his mouth full. He was pretty shocked and didn't want to admit that without Morgan's help he'd really be struggling or that he hadn't exactly been the nicest brother—especially when he accepted Roxanne's praise without giving Morgan any credit. "That would be great," he said, relieved.

Morgan nodded without smiling, and Forrest made a mental note to himself—there was something he needed to talk to Roxanne about.

The siblings hurried down the path from their house to the canine pavilion together.

"I'll get the hose," Forrest said. "Do you want to take them out? Then we can do the food and water?"

Morgan nodded, still feeling a little conflicted. She adored the dogs, of course. But why didn't she just tell her brother what a jerk he'd been last week? Was she a total pushover? She hated that it was so hard for her to stand up for herself.

She let Ember, Bucko, and Woody out of their kennels, leashed them up, and took them outside. They sniffed around and efficiently did their business . . . with the exception of Bucko, who had to find the perfect spot every single time. Round two went more quickly, and then it was time for food and water.

With both of them working, Forrest and Morgan finished the kennel chores in good time, but Forrest couldn't help but notice how gloomy his sister was. He knew he should probably talk to her or say he was sorry, but he didn't want her to pull a Shelby and launch into a long list of everything he had ever done wrong. Besides, he was late. *And* he had a plan he hoped would make it all better. So he kept quiet.

"Thanks, Mor," he said when they were finished. Morgan didn't reply, and Forrest didn't wait—he couldn't. He left the pavilion and jogged out to the outer edges of the ranch. As he approached the area where he had been instructed to "lose" himself, he heard Juniper's high voice calling for Twig. He hoped that his little sister's search wouldn't be another distraction for Ember. He tried to put his worries about his sisters out of his mind and sat down with his back to a tree.

Forrest was used to waiting by now and was smart enough to bring a comic book rolled in his backpack to pass the time. Green Lantern was just about to foil Sinestro for the hundredth time, when Forrest thought he heard Roxanne's familiar command in the distance.

"Find!"

Roxanne stuffed the dirty shirt, Ember's scent article, into a Ziploc bag and watched intently as the dog started her search. Ember seemed a little off today. Overall the Lab was moving well and in the right direction, but she wasn't ranging as far and was pausing more than usual. She even came to a full stop near the handlers' lodge!

Still hiding, Forrest tucked the comic book into his pack and sprawled out on the ground like he was hurt. Soon after, Ember appeared, sat down on her haunches, and barked her alert. Forrest stayed still on the ground and waited for Roxanne, who arrived within thirty seconds . . . more quickly than usual.

"Good girl, Ember," she said, giving her a treat and clipping on her long lead to avoid a repeat of last week.

"You're clear, Forrest," Roxanne said, letting him know he could come out of victim mode. During this late phase, he had to stay still and couldn't even correct Ember on her alert if she didn't do it right. Forrest climbed to his feet, brushing grass and twigs from his backside. "You probably don't need to worry about a lead today since Twig is out of the picture," he half joked.

Roxanne's expression showed her confusion.

"He's missing . . . or at least he didn't show up for breakfast."

"Given that food is the only thing Twig clearly and consistently loves, that's a little distressing," Roxanne said, her brow wrinkling. "Juniper really doesn't know where he is? Those two are practically attached."

Forrest shook his head. "Nope. She spent almost an hour calling him from the back door this morning, and she's checked the house and yard multiple times. She's pretty upset," Forrest admitted. "Dad took her out on a search of the ranch after breakfast."

Suddenly, out of the corner of his eye, Forrest thought he saw something orange flash between some bushes, and in that same instant, Ember took off at full tilt after it, forgetting she was on her lead.

Roxanne braced but was nearly toppled. "Ember, come!" she said, holding her ground. The yellow Lab stopped in her tracks and trotted back guiltily, her tail hanging lower than usual. "Sit," Roxanne said firmly, relieved that she had at least been able to recall the dog. "Three steps forward, two steps back," she muttered under her breath, reminding herself that this was perfectly normal, if a little frustrating.

Ember sat down on her haunches and gazed up at her trainer with her brown eyes full of regret. Roxanne crouched and placed a hand on either side of Ember's face. "Twig or no Twig, what has gotten into you? Where's that laser focus?"

Forrest bit his lip . . . he'd obviously spoken too soon about Ember not needing the lead.

Ember's gaze didn't waver from Roxanne's face. She loved to please her trainer. She loved to find

Forrest. But sometimes her nose got the best of her and told her to do things she wasn't supposed to do, and the tantalizing smell of that cat—and lately something else she couldn't quite identify—was always in the air!

11

"Ember is back on track and nailing it," Forrest announced a week later at the dinner table, his mouth half full of chicken stew. "She's really figuring it all out, and I don't think she'll have any problem with new terrain or more targets or—"

"Don't talk with your mouth full, Forrest," his mother reminded him.

Frances's sharp blue eyes gleamed behind her glasses. "I knew the moment I met that dog that she had loads of potential," she said. "I just wasn't sure how long it would take to get her focused enough to do the work. It can take some dogs months before they start to understand exactly what we are asking them to do."

Juniper thumped her glass of milk on the table. "I don't see how you can talk about Ember's training like nothing is the matter," she complained. "Twig has been gone for an entire week! If one of your precious dogs was missing, everybody would be out looking all day long. You have barely looked for Twig!" She jutted her bottom lip out to further make her point, a tear glistened on her brown cheek.

The rest of the family exchanged a series of looks, and Georgia leaned toward her youngest child. "Liebling," she crooned, smoothing a curl at Juniper's temple. Georgia's first language was Tigrinya, her parents' Eritrean language, but she'd grown up in Germany, where the family first immigrated. Though she'd been in the United States for twenty years, the German word for "darling" often emerged when she was trying to soothe her children.

Juniper leaned in to her mama's hand like a cat and swallowed the rest of her tears.

"I'm sure it seems that way, June Bug," Martin said. "But you and I have been out looking every day, and we have all been keeping an eye peeled for Twig on the ranch."

"And we made signs and put them up in town, remember?" Shelby added. "Almost two dozen of them."

"Yes, and he's still *gone*!" Juniper shoved her plate forward and her chair away from the table, forcing her mom to pull back. "I can't eat . . . or breathe . . . or live!" She faced her family, her eyes welling again with tears and her bottom lip officially wobbling. "I know the truth . . . you all hate him!" While the rest of the family watched in surprise, Juniper stomped out of the dining room and up the stairs.

"I'd say she's pretty upset," Frances announced.

Forrest rolled his eyes. "You mean she's pretty *dramatic*."

"Yes, but Juniper has a point," Martin said with a sigh. "If it was one of the dogs, we'd all be going crazy looking."

"For better or worse, the dogs are our livelihood," Georgia said. "But that doesn't mean we don't love Twig."

Morgan spooned up her last bite of stew and got to her feet. "I'll go talk to her. I don't think she puts me in the 'fully hates Twig' category." She folded her napkin, left her dishes on the table, and took the stairs two at a time. She paused outside Juniper's door, considering what to say. Juniper *was* being irrational, but only because she was so worried. The kid loved Twig more than anything, and it was super easy to worry about something you loved!

Tapping on the door, Morgan asked, "Can I come in?"

The response was a muffled "Mnmhnhh." Morgan turned the knob and peeked into the room. Juniper was lying on her bed, her face pressed into her

106

pillow. Morgan crossed to the bed with its red quilt and propped herself on the edge.

"Twig is a very smart cat," she said, trying not to focus on the missing cat's pillow next to Juniper's at the head of the bed. "He's the smartest cat I know. And he definitely has a mind of his own . . ." She trailed off, not quite sure what to say next. "You know a lot of cats disappear once in a while. It's how they show independence. Twig probably just decided to take a break from all the dogs. Like a cat vacation."

Juniper rolled onto her side and peeked at Morgan through the bend in her arm. "But where could he be?" she asked between sniffles. "And what does he have to eat?" She sniffed an extra-loud sniff. "He's probably starved to death by now!" Juniper lay there for several seconds before adding, "He would never stay away from me this long on purpose!" A fresh wave of tears sprang to her eyes, and she rolled back over, her face resmooshed into her pillow.

A second soft rap on the door interrupted them,

but Juniper didn't move a muscle. "Can I help?" Martin asked.

"Nobody can help!" Juniper's muffled voice was surprisingly loud in the small room. Morgan shook her head at her dad and got to her feet. She gave him an "I tried" shrug.

"Okay, well, I'll be just downstairs if you need me, Bug," her dad said. "And we can go on an after-dinner search walk if you want . . ."

Juniper sat up fast. "Yes, let's!" she said, her blotchy face and puffy eyes giving way to a tiny expression of hope. "Let's *all* go!" She wiped her nose with the back of her hand and looked at her dad and sister.

Martin half smiled at his youngest, who could switch from miserable to excited in the blink of an eye. "If you come eat a bit of dinner, we can round up a crowd when we've all finished," he promised.

Juniper nodded even faster and slid off the bed. "Okay," she said with a sniff.

Morgan looked at her dad with wide eyes. If he

thought he could get Shelby out on a family walk to look for Twig he was sadly mistaken . . . and Forrest was a long shot, too.

With his arm around Juniper, Martin escorted his daughters back to the table, where Forrest was crowing about Ember.

"Roxanne says she's one of the best trackers she's ever trained, she just gets distracted by other smells, especially . . ." He leaned forward, about to say "cats," but stopped himself when he spotted Juniper's damp face. "Other animals," he said instead.

"SAR dogs need to have a mind of their own so they can think for themselves in rescue situations," Forrest went on, waving his fork and acting like he wasn't talking to a table of experts. "So it's a good thing . . . except for when it isn't. She's really coming along, though. It's amazing!"

Morgan scowled at her plate. She hated hearing Forrest go on and on like he was in charge of training. It was like he was trying to rub her face in it.

And he acted so proud—like it was all his doing. All he had to do was *hide*! It was almost like he was trying to take the credit for Ember's hard work, and Roxanne's, just like he'd been taking credit for hers. Sometimes Forrest was such a jerk. She started to open her mouth to tell him exactly what she thought, when a voice interrupted them from the front hall.

"Hello?" Roxanne called out to the family. Martin and Georgia stood to welcome her as she appeared around the corner. When Roxanne saw that they were eating, she shook her head. "Oh. Sorry to interrupt dinner."

"Don't be silly. You're always welcome," Georgia replied, pulling up an extra chair. She had a way of making everyone who walked in the door feel like part of the family. "Are you hungry? Do you want some food? Coffee?" Georgia roasted her own coffee beans on the stove every morning and each night before dinner and was always ready to make a fresh pot.

Roxanne patted her belly. "No food. I just ate waaayyy too many tacos in town," she said. "But you know I can't resist your coffee." Georgia smiled and went to fetch a cup while Roxanne's eyes settled on Morgan. The trainer smiled. "I was actually hoping to talk to Morgan here for a minute."

Morgan's head shot up. Was she in trouble? Had she forgotten to put one of the training logs back? Sometimes she borrowed them without permission so she could study up on what the dogs were working on and the different training challenges . . .

Georgia came back into the dining room and handed Roxanne a small steaming cup. The super-fresh brew was the only coffee Roxanne liked without cream and sugar.

"Can I talk to Morgan outside?" she asked after thanking Georgia and enjoying a hot sip.

Martin and Georgia nodded in unison at Roxanne. "Of course," Georgia replied. "Morgan, as soon as you're—"

"I'm done!" Morgan nervously got to her feet and grabbed her plate, clearing it quickly and banging her knee in the process. She ignored the pain, set her dish in the kitchen sink with a clatter, and followed Roxanne outside. Simultaneously grateful to leave the table and nervous about what Roxanne wanted to talk to her about, she reminded herself to breathe.

Outside, the sky was a clear cobalt blue. Since the days were still summertime long, the sun hadn't yet dipped behind the horizon.

"Let's talk over here." Roxanne walked over to the picnic table in the backyard, and Morgan followed like a new dog in training, not knowing what was coming next. Instead of sitting down, she shifted from one foot to the other, waiting for Roxanne to speak.

"I have a favor to ask you."

Morgan stopped shifting and looked up in surprise. "A favor?" she echoed.

"Yes. I need a second training helper for Ember . . .

a decoy—somebody new to hide on the trail—to try and throw her off. She's getting closer to certification every week, but her distractibility is still a bit of an issue. We need to really test it."

Morgan nodded. She'd read about that. It seemed almost mean, in a way, to try to trick a dog in training. But it was important to know how they would react in the field with a bazillion unknowns. "Ooookay," Morgan said slowly. She was confused why Roxanne was telling her this. She usually talked over training stuff with Pedro or one of the other trainers. Roxanne and Pedro worked together like right and left hand, so . . .

"I was hoping it could be you," Roxanne finished.

Morgan's mouth dropped open.

A small smile played on Roxanne's lips before they disappeared into her coffee cup, and Morgan wondered if she knew what this meant to her. Her heart felt like it might leap right out of her chest with happiness!

"I'd love to!" she cried, throwing her arms around Roxanne. "Thank you!"

Roxanne put her hand on Morgan's shoulder and gave it a warm squeeze. "You deserve it, Morgan. You're not a big talker, but I see how you love the dogs, how good you are with them, and how hard you work. Forrest told me how much you've been helping him with the pavilion chores, too. In fact, he's the one who suggested I ask you. As soon as he said it aloud, I knew he was right. I think you're ready for the responsibility."

Morgan pulled back and nodded, surprised for a second time. *Forrest* told Roxanne that she'd been helping? *He* suggested that she be another training assistant? She definitely wasn't expecting that! She smiled to herself. It was a good thing she didn't tell him off at the dinner table!

12

Morgan hopped out of bed, her whole body smiling, and pulled on a pair of shorts and a T-shirt. Today was her first day as a training assistant! Finally! She rushed down the hall to find the bathroom occupied, and rapped on the door impatiently.

"Just a sec!" came a voice from the other side. The door swung open and Juniper's expectant face peered at her.

"Are you ready?" Juniper asked.

Morgan racked her brain . . . ready for what? For a split second, she thought Juniper was asking if she was ready to help with training. But she hadn't told her about that. She hadn't told anyone. She was hanging on to that information like a birthday wish, as if telling somebody might keep it from coming true.

"I know we'll find Twig today. I just know it!" Juniper said. Her voice wasn't as hopeful as her words.

Morgan gulped.

A few nights ago, when they'd gone out after dinner to look for the cat (a search Morgan barely remembered because she was floating on cloud nine), she and her dad had said they'd help keep looking until they found him. She hadn't meant every single day, though. She had another commitment this morning . . . one she'd been waiting for forever!

"Can't," she said, pushing into the bathroom and pulling off her sleep cap in front of the mirror. "I have to do the morning dog care, and then I get to help Roxanne and Forrest train Ember." She twirled some of the short twists that had loosened during the night.

It took less than one second for Juniper's face to bunch up like a wet, moldy rag. "You're helping with that . . . that menace?" she challenged.

Morgan blinked, realizing she should have apologized, or at least given Juniper the news a little more gently. "Well . . ." she mumbled.

Juniper crossed her arms over her chest and jutted a hip against the door. "Of course you are! Nobody around here cares about my cat." She raised her chin defiantly even as it started to wobble. "Or me!"

Morgan exhaled. "I can't help it . . . I promised I'd . . ."

"I'll just go find him myself!" Juniper hissed, uncrossing her arms to shove Morgan back into the hallway. "And you can find another bathroom!" she added, slamming the door in Morgan's face.

Morgan sighed and stepped back from the door, which had stopped just inches from her nose. She felt bad but was also annoyed. Her little sister was such a drama queen! She wanted to shout at her through the door, but her bladder told her there was no time for that, so she dashed down the stairs to the half bath off the kitchen instead.

When Morgan got to the pavilion, she was first to arrive, but barely.

"Morning!" Forrest practically chirped as he came through the door a few minutes behind her. "Thanks for coming to help!"

"Who are you, and what have you done with my brother?" Morgan asked, trying to look stern.

Forrest broke into a grin, displaying the gap in his teeth. "You'll never know . . ." Forrest replied, picking up the hose and waving it in her direction.

Ember let out a bark from inside her kennel, reminding them why they were there, and the two got to work.

"I'll hose down the kennels today," Morgan said, slipping her sneakered feet into a giant pair of rubber boots and taking the hose from her brother. "You walk the pups."

Forrest nodded, and they began the washing, walking, watering, and feeding. They finished quickly and used the extra time to start a load of dog towels and blankets in the washing machine that their dad had installed in the pavilion for just that purpose. When they stepped outside, Roxanne was coming up the path.

"Oh good, you're both here," she said. "Forrest, I'd like you to go hide out by Pedro's trailer." Forrest smiled. Pedro lived in a decked-out trailer on the far end of the ranch. Pedro spent a lot of time fielding calls from people and organizations all over the world looking for dogs to join their rescue teams . . . whether it was an individual in a small town, a ranger, a firefighter, or the coast guard. He had an uncanny ability to read people, even over the phone, and was equally good at matching the dogs who were about to be certified with the right handlers. He also had an appreciation for soda and snack foods, and kept an ample supply of both in the vintage fridge on his covered porch . . .

"And no sneaking soda and chips from his stash," Roxanne added with a wink.

Forrest blinked in surprise—she'd basically read his mind! He covered his mischievous smirk with his hand and nodded. "Got it," he replied, taking off at a jog.

"Morgan, I want you to hide next to the rubble pile, but on the far side." The rubble pile was probably the biggest feature on the ranch since it was used for both agility and disaster training. As facilities manager, it was Martin's job to keep it piled high with all kinds of different building materials . . . everything from old two-by-fours to cement blocks to pipes and other construction debris. The heap was constantly changing to keep the dogs on their toes . . . literally. "Follow Forrest's path until you reach the second shade structure. We're hoping Ember will ignore your trail when it splits off and stick with the one she's supposed to be following . . . Forrest's."

Morgan's smile was wide as she trotted after her

brother. She felt like the moment she had been waiting for her entire life was finally arriving—or almost. What she really wanted to do was be the person in charge of training, like Roxanne. Someday . . .

When she reached the second shade structure, Morgan veered and made a beeline to the rubble pile, which had grown since the last time she saw it. She walked around to the back, where she was out of sight of the path, and squatted down between some cement blocks and a heap of discarded wooden pallets.

Roxanne waited back at the pavilion for a good twenty minutes to make sure Forrest and Morgan had enough time to get situated. She kept Ember sitting calmly by her side and practiced continued eye contact, two exercises that were initially a challenge for the energetic pup but were definitely easier now.

Roxanne pulled a scent article out of her pack and removed it from the plastic bag. She had been using less and less smelly items through the course of the training to strengthen Ember's scenting skills.

Out in the field, a dog might have to track with a very small amount of odor, or on a very old trail, and Roxanne had learned the hard way that a dog accustomed to super-smelly socks or sweaty T-shirts would have a tougher time sticking to older and more subtle scents. To get Ember ready for anything, she'd started using shorts that had been worn and then washed, or shoes that hadn't had feet in them for several weeks.

"Here, Ember," Roxanne said, holding out a pair of Forrest's clean soccer shorts. Ember had learned that this part was important, and she took her time sniffing the shorts, burying her snout into the folds of the fabric.

Ember waited, proud in her SAR vest, for the command she loved. She had grown to anticipate it so much that sometimes it was hard to be patient! Finally, it came.

"Find!"

Ember dropped her head to the ground and sniffed her way along the path taken by the Sterling kids, scenting both of them as she trotted forward at a steady pace. Within a few minutes, she had arrived at the second shade structure, where the scent trails split. Ember paused. She recognized Morgan's smell and was tempted to track the girl down. The smell was comforting . . . and it wasn't usually there during training! But the smell on the shorts Roxanne held out for her was twelve-year-old boy, Forrest. That was what she was supposed to find, and she knew it. With only a brief pause and a glance in the other direction, she continued tracking the boy.

Following behind, Roxanne could hardly believe this was the same dog she'd met just months ago, or even the distractible dog of last week! Nearly every dog was trainable, but Ember was particularly eager to learn, and when she was focused, she was one of the fastest trackers Roxanne had ever worked with.

Out beyond Pedro's trailer, Forrest skipped the comic book and just lay on his back and watched the clouds. He didn't have to wait long. When Ember found him, she calmly sat down on her haunches and barked her alert. Forrest cheered inside, thrilled to be able to watch this process, and Ember's success. Roxanne was so knowledgeable, and Ember was soaking up her teachings like a sponge. Ember longed to do the right thing . . . and was doing it! Forrest looked at his watch. Case in point: Only thirty-three minutes had passed since he'd left Roxanne, Ember, and his sister by the pavilion. At this rate, Ember would definitely be ready to be matched with a handler and get her certification before the end of summer!

13

After three more hide-and-seek sessions, which Ember aced, Roxanne, Forrest, and Morgan made their way back to the kennels.

"It's funny how I never got to see Ember out there, but I still felt involved in this morning's training," Morgan said.

Roxanne nodded. "There are so many components to a training session, and each one is important. We learned a lot about Ember's increased ability to focus today, and you helped make that happen."

Morgan felt a little thrill at the compliment, and

also just plain happy. A tiny part of her had hoped the pup would find her at least once so they would need more practice and she'd get to work on the training team longer, but celebrating Ember's success was more fun . . . and more important.

"Who's a good dog?" Morgan asked, skipping alongside Ember. She patted her leg and ran a few steps ahead. Ember bounded after her, but they both stopped short when they heard someone coming toward them and wailing.

It was Juniper, of course, and Morgan immediately saw the reason why she was crying. Twig's collar was clutched in her hand . . . with no Twig to go with it.

"It was on the fence by the road!" Juniper sobbed. She spun and shouted at Ember, getting close to her face. "And it's all your fault, you stupid dog!" she spat angrily.

Ember stopped wagging her tail. She backed away from Juniper, her ears flat and her tail down. She was getting the "bad dog" message loud and clear.

"Juniper, don't shout at Ember," Roxanne said sternly, stepping between them. "First of all, it's not fair. Ember didn't send Twig away. Ember is a dog being a dog, and Twig is a cat being a cat. And second, you should never get in a dog's face like that. You're threatening her, and she might decide she needs to defend herself."

Juniper stood taller for about two seconds and then appeared to shrink. She wiped her cheek with the back of her hand, leaving a streak of dirt, and drew a ragged breath. Her face revealed equal parts anger, sadness, and guilt. Morgan half expected her to lash out again, but instead Juniper hung her head.

"I know," she said, a fresh wash of tears erupting from her eyes. "I'm sorry. I just . . . I just want Twig to come home. I want him to be okay."

Morgan put her arm over her sister's shoulders, which felt smaller than usual. Juniper drew in a jerky breath. Morgan felt terrible for not being nicer this morning, and for not helping search. She probably couldn't have changed the outcome, but maybe if she'd been there when Juniper found the collar she could have . . . she wasn't even sure what.

"I know, June. I want to find Twig, too. We all do." She gently steered her sister toward the house. "Let me make you a grilled cheese, and then we can go on a search together. The collar doesn't mean anything . . . Twig hates that thing. You know the bell on it keeps him from being able to hunt birds. He's lost it on purpose lots of times. It kind of explains why we haven't heard him."

Juniper sniffled loudly and nodded. She knew. And grilled cheese was her absolute favorite food. "With no crust?" she asked weakly.

Morgan's dark eyes sparkled knowingly. Even when her little sister was upset, she was a negotiator. "Not a single bite of crust, and extra cheddar." Juniper smiled a tiny smile, and the two made their way to the house with Morgan's arm still draped over her little sister's shoulders. But despite Morgan's grilled cheese perfection, Juniper only swallowed a few bites. She was shoving her plate away when Forrest barreled through the door.

"I'll take that," he said, snatching up her leftovers and eating half in one bite.

Morgan shot him a look as she wrapped up the cheddar and put it back in the fridge. "Does that mean you're going to help us look for Twig this afternoon?" she asked pointedly.

Forrest started to say he couldn't, but Morgan's gaze of steel made him reconsider.

"I'll do it if you make me a grilled cheese and tomato," he bargained. "I have a couple of hours before I meet the guys for soccer."

"Fine," Morgan agreed, taking the cheese back out of the fridge.

"Did you ask Shelby, too?" Forrest wanted to know.

"She's working the front desk," Juniper said. "Which means she's on her phone." She did a quick imitation of Shelby as a cell phone zombie, eyes crossed and fingers flying on an invisible screen.

Morgan buttered two more slices of bread. She remembered when her sister used to talk to her instead of her friends, but those days were gone. She piled one slice of bread with cheese and added a thick slice of tomato. Forrest peered over her shoulder eagerly—Juniper wasn't the only grilled cheese lover, and Morgan had it down. A few minutes later, she slipped a golden-brown sandwich onto a plate.

"Thanks, Mor," Forrest said. He bit into it immediately, nearly burning the roof of his mouth.

"I'm going to get cat treats," Juniper said, hopping off her chair. She disappeared into the back hall and returned with a backpack jammed with every cat treat she could find in the Sterling pantry—more than a whole clowder of cats could eat in a sitting. "I bet he's really hungry," Juniper said, catching her sister's look. Morgan hoped so.

When Forrest finished eating, the three set out. They walked the edge of the property, zigzagging in and out to search the mock plane crash site, the rubble pile, and the area behind Pedro's trailer.

"Heeeerrrre, Twiggy Twig," Juniper called, over and over, while she and Forrest crisscrossed paths, trying to cover as much ground as possible.

Given how upset Juniper had been earlier, Morgan thought she was doing a good job staying calm. She was trying to stay calm herself, to soothe her sister, but inside she felt agitated. And worried. In spite of what she'd said about Twig's bell alerting the birds, finding Twig's collar wasn't a good sign, and she worried that they might find something else they really didn't want to . . . like Twig's body.

"See anything?" Forrest asked, jogging up to her. His hair had gotten long over the summer, and he shook it back out of his eyes.

"Nothing," Morgan said in a near whisper while

she watched her little sister push aside some branches at the base of a cluster of bushes, practically crawling under the shrubbery. "It's like finding a needle in a haystack," she said softly. The ranch was huge. Twig was small. He could be anywhere.

Forrest nodded. "I have a feeling Twig doesn't want to be found. Or maybe he's—"

"Shhhhh!" Morgan shushed him before he could say it. Forrest was afraid of the same thing she was. She tilted her head toward Juniper, signaling. "Don't even say that out loud," she whispered. They both knew that cats sometimes wandered off to die alone when they were old or sick. But Twig was neither of these things.

Forrest nodded again. "But . . . he's been gone for a week, and nobody has responded to the signs in town. And now the collar . . ." He trailed off and kicked at a pebble on the ground with his sneaker.

"I know, just please don't let Juniper hear that—it would freak her out."

"She's already freaked out, but . . . yeah . . . you're right." With a collective sigh of disappointment, they turned past Pedro's trailer and started back to the canine pavilion.

14

That night, Morgan couldn't sleep. She tossed and turned well past midnight, picturing Juniper's face at dinner. Their search had turned up nothing, and though Morgan and Forrest were glad they hadn't found a body, Juniper's switch from angry and upset to shutting down was hard to watch. Their hyper-dramatic sister was starting to seem like a robot, like nothing mattered now that Twig was gone.

Morgan rolled over for the zillionth time and turned her pillow to the cool side before punching it in frustration. She just wanted to sleep! Then, as she was about to put her head back down, she had an idea, a brilliant idea. She could use Ember to find Twig! The two animals clearly had some kind of connection, so who better to track down the missing cat than a trained tracking dog with a cat fascination? It was so obvious and so smart she wondered why she hadn't thought of it before!

Morgan stared at the ceiling and considered her plan. She couldn't deny that it broke a lot of rules. She wasn't Ember's trainer, for one. She wasn't even Ember's victim! She was just a helper and a decoy. And yet . . .

After listening to make sure Shelby's breathing in the next bed was deep and regular, Morgan stopped thinking and threw herself into action . . . quietly. She lifted her covers aside and climbed stealthily out of bed. Her clothing options were limited since she didn't want to risk opening her dresser or the closet, so she pulled on the pants and long sweatshirt she'd left on the chair by her bed. She tiptoed out of their room and down the hall, pausing to listen at Juniper's door until she could make out her little sister's snores. Grateful for the noise, Morgan crept into Juniper's room and slipped Twig's pillow off the bed. After backing into the hallway and closing the door with a soft click, she carried the pillow downstairs and shoved it into the backpack in the hall. She chose one of the headlamps her dad kept hanging on the inside of the closet door and tested the light to make sure the batteries were good. Finally she grabbed her shoes and crept outside. The door clicked shut, and she breathed a heavy sigh of relief. She was one step closer to finding Twig and making things right!

Morgan pulled on her sneakers without untying them and walked as noiselessly as she could toward the pavilion. She was hyperaware of every single sound—the crunching gravel, the snapping sticks, the crickets. She shivered, though it wasn't cold. When she was about halfway there—between the pools of light provided by the buildings—she turned on her headlamp, keeping it switched to low. The pavilion door was unlocked, and Ember lifted her sleepy head and wagged like mad as soon as she smelled Morgan. Several of the other dogs whined sleepily, too.

"Shhhhh," Morgan told them. "We've got to be quiet." The last thing she wanted was to start the dogs barking and bring everyone running to see what was going on.

Ember read Morgan loud and clear. Though the girl usually came when the sun was first up to pet and feed her, right now she was there for work. Ember walked calmly through the kennel door when Morgan unlatched it and stood perfectly still while the girl strapped on her SAR vest.

"I hope that's right," Morgan whispered to Ember in the dark. "This thing is more complicated than it looks!" Morgan tugged on the straps until the vest felt secure and then clipped on Ember's long lead. They walked softly on feet and paws to the door and were soon outside in the dark of night. The sky was overcast, but Morgan could make out the almost full moon behind the clouds. She was glad she'd thought to bring the headlamp! She led Ember a short distance away and asked her to sit.

"Stay," she said. Ember did as she was told. She didn't move while Morgan pulled Twig's pillow from her backpack, but watched the girl's every move. Morgan held out the pillow, and Ember sniffed it from edge to edge, excitedly inhaling. The pillow was ripe with the scent Ember had been wanting to track, the one that kept distracting her when she was supposed to be finding twelve-year-old boy!

Morgan sensed Ember's excitement and felt a thrill of anticipation herself. "Let's hope this works!" she whispered. She put the pillow back in her backpack and focused on Ember. The dog was gazing at her expectantly, waiting for her command.

"Find!" she said, and Ember didn't need to hear it twice.

Morgan followed in the dark, expecting Ember

to lead her toward the fence where Juniper found the collar. Then she checked herself. Handlers were not supposed to anticipate their dogs' actions. She stopped, letting the lead tighten, and forced herself to stop guessing what Ember would do. Dogs were often so anxious to please that their handlers had to avoid "suggesting" any outcomes to their dogs . . . even with body language! Morgan had to allow Ember to do the searching, the work she was trained to do. She had to let Ember lead.

Taking a breath, Morgan tried to simply follow Ember, who was making a zigzag path in order to find a trail. Finally she stopped darting back and forth and seemed to settle on a direction. At the handlers' lodge, Ember made a clear turn toward the maintenance annex a few hundred yards away. The maintenance annex was the building where Morgan's dad stored wood and paint and tools and fencing—whatever he needed to keep the ranch in working order. There were a lot of strong smells in the barn-sized building, even for a human! Ember sniffed her way to the entrance, then sat down and let out a bark.

"Shhhh!" Morgan said with a start. The noise sounded crazy loud in the quiet of night. But in a flash Morgan realized Ember was just doing her job. "Sorry. I didn't mean that. I mean, uh, . . . good dog," she corrected, giving Ember a pet.

She looked around. Ember had alerted her, but . . . there was no Twig. No cat. Maybe Ember was confused. Morgan stood still for several seconds, wondering if she had done something wrong, if she'd led Ember astray somehow. Then she looked at the dog, who was still sitting calmly. She was looking at the annex door. "Really, Ember? Here?" Morgan asked. She listened in the darkness, as if Ember could answer her in English.

"What are you doing?" a voice whispered, echoing Morgan's own doubts.

Morgan jumped and spun around. The beam from

her headlamp caught her older sister right in the eye. Shelby squinted and threw up her hand to block the light.

"I could ask you the same question," Morgan shot back defensively. "Are you following me?"

"You woke me up when you left, Godzilla. I thought you were just stomping down to the bathroom, but when I didn't hear a flush and *did* hear the back door open, I looked out the window and saw your head-lamp. So, yeah, I followed to see what you are up to." She crossed her arms and tried to look tough in paja-mas. "So, Morgan Sterling . . . what *are* you up to?"

"Ummmm . . ." Morgan was tongue-tied.

"I hope you're looking for the mysterious disap-pearing cat Juniper is freaking about. That girl is seriously ruining my summer!"

Relief washed over Morgan, even as Ember nosed her knee, clearly confused. She sniffed Morgan's pocket, looking for a treat. Hadn't she led Morgan to the place with the smell?

When Morgan didn't respond, Ember decided that the search was over, treat or no treat, and walked over to greet Shelby and lick her hand.

"Who's a good girl?" Shelby crooned, crouching down in front of the yellow Lab.

"Stop petting her!" Morgan whispered hoarsely. According to her reading, Ember might be puzzled by excess praise and petting while she was working. "You're just confusing her. You have to leave until she finds her target. And there's only supposed to be one person telling her what to do."

Shelby's eyes widened, and she cocked her pink-streaked head—she didn't like being bossed around by her younger siblings. If there was someone telling anyone else what to do, she preferred it to be *her*. "Who do you think you—"

Morgan squared her shoulders. "Do you want us to find Twig, or not?"

"Okay, fine. I'll let you get back to your search," Shelby huffed. To show her annoyance, she gave

Ember a final pet before turning on her heels and storming back toward the house in her slippers. Morgan watched her go, wondering which of her sisters was more dramatic . . . Juniper or Shelby.

When Shelby was completely out of sight, Morgan pulled Twig's pillow out of her pack once more and let Ember get another good sniff. Ember didn't take as long to get the scent this time, and before Morgan could put the pillow back, Ember sat down and let out another sharp bark, as if she'd just arrived at the door. She was definitely alerting her, even though there was no cat. "So Twig's inside?" Morgan asked.

She stepped closer to the building and pulled on the heavy lock that held the double doors closed from the outside. It was latched tightly. Morgan tapped her toe on the ground, thinking. Her parents had keys . . . maybe it hadn't been such a great idea to send Shelby packing so quickly. She could have asked her to go get them!

"Oh well," Morgan whispered. She'd have to go get

them herself. She started toward the house, expecting Ember to follow, but the yellow dog began walking in the other direction with her nose close to the ground.

"Ember, come!" Morgan shined her headlamp on the dog. Ember didn't even turn . . . she just kept going. Morgan flung her hands out in exasperation.

"Fine, we'll go the loooong way around," she groused, following Ember around the corner. Halfway down the long side of the building, Ember stopped again beneath a large window. She stuck her nose up to the opening and sniffed for a couple seconds, and barked.

"Here?" Morgan asked. She wished Ember's alerts weren't so loud . . . but of course they had to be.

She looked at the large window that Ember was focused on. It was open and hinged in the middle, with the bottom edge pushed out toward them and the top swinging into the large, dark building. Unfortunately, the window had a mechanism that prevented it from opening more than forty-five degrees, but by turning to the side, Morgan was able to get her head through the gap and lift her chin above the sill so her headlamp could shine into the cavernous room.

She saw stacks of wood, tall metal shelves, and lots of tools hanging on the wall, but no cat. If Twig were in there, he'd probably be hiding under something, anyway. Morgan was pretty slight but still didn't think her whole body would fit through the opening. Ember's might, though . . .

Morgan pulled her head back out and considered the situation. Should she let Ember go in without her? Go find the keys to unlock the door? Or both?

She made the decision quickly. Patting the window ledge, she gave the command quietly but firmly. "Find!"

Ember put her front paws on the sill, kicked off, and wiggled into the opening, sliding her body through like a seal. Morgan put her own head back through the window and watched Ember sniff her way around the room before disappearing behind some shelves and beyond the shaft of light thrown by the headlamp. Ember was on her way . . . and on her own.

15

As soon as she lost sight of Ember, Morgan ducked her head back out of the window gap and ran toward the house. When she could see the light shining on the back porch, she reached up, turned off her headlamp, and slowed to a walk. The last thing she wanted was for her parents to wake up now, before she'd successfully executed her plan.

Luckily the pegs where the family hung their keys were just inside the back door, and her father's key ring was easy to feel for. It was by far the largest—he had to have access to every building on the ranch. It was also, unfortunately, the jingliest.

Morgan wrapped the keys in her shirt to muffle their noise and stepped back out onto the porch. She closed the door as quietly as she could, flinching when the latch clicked. She waited for a beat, holding still and not breathing, to listen for stirrings inside the house. When she didn't hear anything, she hurried down the three steps and off the porch, holding tightly to the key ring to keep it quiet. As soon as she was far enough away, she broke into a run.

By the time she got back to the maintenance annex door, she was out of breath. She panted, leaned against the door, and looked down at the dozens of keys in the beam of her headlamp. There had to be fifty at least! And none of them were labeled. She blew a long, slow breath out her nose. There was only one way to figure out which one would open the padlock . . . she was going to have to try them all, one by one.

"I'm coming, Ember," she whispered, hoping the dog wasn't as scared in the dark maintenance building all alone as she would be.

The first three keys didn't fit at all. The fourth went in but wouldn't turn. Morgan was trying the seventh key (and trying not to curse) when her hand slipped and she dropped the ring. The keys splayed in the dust, and she had no way to tell which of them she'd already tested.

"Are you kidding me?" she asked the darkness. She started over, this time making it through all the keys. Several of them went into the lock, but once inside she could not make any of them budge. Morgan was certain one of the keys on the ring had to open the lock. She just couldn't figure out which!

With a sigh, she tucked the oversized ring into her back pocket and jogged back to the open window.

"Ember?" she called softly. The dog did not come. "Ember," she called again, as loudly as she dared. When the yellow Lab still didn't appear, she felt panic rise like a tide inside her, swelling up from her stomach and into her throat. "Ember, come!" she called once more. She tried to sound firm like Roxanne but could hear the fear in her own voice.

Suddenly Morgan's good idea was not feeling so good. She fought back her worries. What if she'd put Ember in danger? There were a lot of toxic things in the annex. She wouldn't be able to live with herself if Ember got hurt or sick because of her. She was trying to help . . . not make things worse!

"Okay, you've got this," Morgan whispered, giving herself a pep talk. "If Ember won't come to you, you have to go to her."

Morgan looked at the window opening again. She reached inside, feeling all around on the interior walls, grasping for handholds. She thought maybe if she found a good hold and entered headfirst like Ember had, she might be able to get inside.

"Mmmph." She found an edge to grab with her left hand and kicked off from the ground with her feet. She made it partway through the opening and stopped. Her hips were stuck. She shimmied them through the narrow passage and then tumbled headlong into the workroom, hitting the sawdust-covered floor at the same time something landed outside with a loud jingle—the ring of keys.

16

"Good morning!" Georgia opened the back door with her second cup of coffee in one hand. She wore a wide smile and her long black curls swept into a loose bun. "Would you like some coffee?" she greeted Pedro with a one-arm hug.

Pedro returned Georgia's hug and stepped inside the cozy kitchen. "Sí, I'd love some," he told her. He removed the cowboy hat he always wore when he worked outside and ran a hand over his graying hair, making it stand up before taking a seat at the kitchen table. He loved meeting with Georgia, who was technically his boss, at her house. The Sterling kitchen was often chaotic—with four kids, there was always something happening—and it reminded him of his own family growing up. He was one of seven, and the commotion was familiar. It was one of the things that he loved best about working for the center—that it felt like home.

Today things in the Sterling household seemed fairly calm, partially due to the fact that not one of the children was in the kitchen.

"Roxanne should be here soon," Georgia said, delivering Pedro's steaming cup of coffee. Pedro nodded and helped himself to two heaping spoonfuls of sugar.

Georgia smiled into her mug. Pedro's sweet tooth was no secret—he liked candy as much as her kids did. And she knew if she turned away he'd happily slip in a third and fourth spoonful of sugar. But his sugar crush was the only childish thing about Pedro—ever since he'd come to work at the ranch, things had gotten easier, especially for Georgia. Pedro was exceptionally skilled at his job. He had a remarkable way with the handlers he trained. With Pedro looking out for the people and Roxanne looking out for the dogs and the other trainers, Georgia felt like she had found the dream team. And truth be told, they all agreed that humans were the hardest animals to train.

"Sorry I'm late." Roxanne walked through the back door without knocking. She felt badly about showing up last for the meeting Pedro had requested. "You wanted to talk about Ember?"

Georgia stood to give Roxanne a hug and get a third cup of coffee.

"Yes." Pedro nodded and folded his hands on the table. "I was wondering how she's coming along. The handlers I'm working with are all doing really well, and that firefighter I mentioned, the one who lives in the mountains—" Pedro stopped. He struggled to find the right words to describe the guy.

"I think he's going to need *just* the right dog, and I think your yellow Lab might be the one, if she'll be ready. Unfortunately my guy can't stick around long because fire season starts soon and with the lack of rain we've had this year they're gonna need him."

Roxanne sipped her coffee and nodded thoughtfully. "Ember is *almost* ready," she said. She was about to ask Pedro more about the firefighter when Forrest bounded into the kitchen.

"Ember is *totally* ready!" he hooted. "I mean. Sorry for listening in. But you should have seen her yesterday! She's—"

Georgia turned her usually warm brown eyes on her son, giving him a cooling look. Forrest clamped his mouth shut in a hurry. Ember's "readiness" was not his call. And he knew better than to interrupt a meeting of adults.

"I agree with Forrest, actually," Roxanne said, a corner of her mouth rising at his enthusiasm. "Ember is going to make a fine SAR dog. I think I'm just a little more cautious than my assistant," she added with a flick of her eyebrows. Then she looked at her phone. "Hey, aren't you running a little late?" she asked Forrest.

Forrest grimaced. He was always running a little late! But most of the time Roxanne wasn't in the kitchen to see it. "Oops!" he said sheepishly. He grabbed his toast out of the toaster and slathered it with peanut butter. "Has anyone seen Morgan?" he asked with his mouth full. She was usually finishing her cereal by the time he made it to the kitchen, but the chair she liked by the window was empty.

The adults at the table all shook their heads.

"Maybe she's already at the pavilion." Forrest waved with one hand, clutched his to-go breakfast in the other, and jammed his feet into his sneakers. He then shuffled out the door.

The door had just slammed shut when Shelby came into the kitchen, staring at her phone. Juniper was right behind her and looking like a dark storm cloud. Stray hairs were springing loose from her braids, and she was scowling at the floor. Clearly, Twig had not come home.

"Was that Morgan?" Shelby asked, lifting her chin toward the back door and taking a seat beside Roxanne.

Georgia held out her hand to her eldest. "No phones at the table," she said. It was a familiar rule. Shelby handed it over with a heavy sigh, and Roxanne slid her own phone into her pocket sheepishly.

"That was your brother," Georgia said as she stowed the phone in a basket on the counter. "I haven't seen Morgan this morning."

"That's weird." Shelby furrowed her brow. "I didn't hear her get up." She tried to look unconcerned as she took a banana from the bowl of fruit in the middle of the table, but her stomach did a funny flip. She hadn't heard Morgan come back to bed last night, either.

"She's gone!"

The crowd around the table heard Forrest before they saw him. He flung open the back door, out of breath. "She's gone," he repeated.

Shelby's flipping stomach jumped to her throat. "Morgan?" she asked.

"No. Ember! She's not in her kennel!" Forrest looked from his mom to Roxanne to Pedro.

"What's going on?" Martin appeared in the other doorway and Juniper rushed to her dad.

"Everyone's disappearing!" Juniper wailed. "Twig, that maniac dog . . ."

"Morgan . . ." Shelby muttered softly.

"Yeah, and my keys," Martin added. He put his hand on Juniper's head, and she buried her face in his shirt while he chewed his lower lip, thinking. Juniper was dramatic. Not *everything* was gone, but it was an odd coincidence to have so many things missing at once. He looked around the room. The other adults shared the same wrinkled foreheads and concerned looks.

Shelby was staring at the table. She bit her lips together and blinked slowly. Then she looked up at her mom and dad and heaved a huge sigh. "I think I know where to find at least two of our missing things . . ."

Still dressed in pajamas, Shelby slipped on a pair of flip-flops and led the whole gang out the back door and along the path she'd followed Morgan's headlamp down the night before. She hoped Morgan would forgive her for telling their parents that she'd snuck out. But even if she was mad, Shelby had to come clean, she was honestly worried. It didn't make sense that Morgan hadn't put Ember away and come back to bed. She hoped her sister—and Ember— were okay. She wished she had never left them alone.

"This is where I saw them last night," Shelby said when they reached the doors to the maintenance annex. She stared at her feet as she said it, unable to look her parents in the eyes.

"What? You were *out* last night?" Georgia folded

159

her arms across her chest and was about to launch into a lecture when Forrest called them from around the corner.

"You guys! Over here! Dad! I found your keys!" he shouted. He had followed the dog prints in the dust to the open window where the keys were lying on the ground. "They were under the window, but—"

Martin squinted at the window, then hurried with his heavy key ring back to the locked doors. He found the right key immediately but struggled to turn it. "If Morgan was trying to get in, she might have had some trouble. I've been meaning to squirt a little WD-40 in here."

The key finally turned, and Martin pulled the lock down, twisting and removing it in one fluid motion. He swung the doors wide, and everyone stepped into the big work space.

"Ember?" Forrest called.

"Twig?" Juniper shouted.

"Morgan, get your butt out here!" Shelby yelled

loudest of all. She was not going to take the fall for her sister's late-night shenanigans—not alone, anyway!

There was no answer, but from deep in the large room, the search crew heard a rustling noise and they all walked toward it, taking different paths through the maze of tall shelves.

"Oh!" Georgia gasped when she saw Morgan's sneakers and striped socks sticking out from underneath the painting workbench. As soon as she realized the girl had not been crushed, she put her hand up to hide her smile—her middle daughter's legs looked like the Wicked Witch of the East's legs sticking out from under the fallen house in *The Wizard of Oz*, only Morgan was not wicked . . . just disobedient.

Georgia crouched down and her small smile broke into a huge grin, then a guffaw. She laughed with amusement and relief at the menagerie beneath the bench: a yawning girl, a yellow dog, a grumpy old tomcat . . . and a litter of tiny kittens all blinking sleepily out at her.

17

"Twig, you are a HERO!" Juniper spun around in the big dusty room with the cranky-looking orange tabby in her outstretched arms. She pulled the cat to her chest and kissed the top of his head. "And you're a *daddy*! And maybe a *mommy*, too!"

As soon as her mother had spotted Twig under the painting bench with the strange cast of critters, Juniper had crawled in and snatched out her beloved kitty. She was ecstatic to have Twig back and bursting with pride over the fact that it seemed he had disappeared in order to take care of a litter of five orphaned kittens!

"I knew you wouldn't leave me for no reason!" Juniper crowed, giving him another kiss.

"How do you know Twig was caring for those kittens?" Shelby asked.

"I know because I know!" Juniper replied gleefully. "Cats do that, you know. They'll take care of a litter that's not theirs if something happens to the mom."

"Isn't it usually another mama cat that takes over?" Shelby asked.

Juniper turned away from her oldest sister. "Yes, but Twiggy is exceptional," she said, offended. She started to storm out, but her dad stepped into her path.

"Slow down, June Bug," Martin said. "First of all, we don't know that the mama cat isn't around somewhere and planning to return. Second, you can't take Twig away if he really is caring for these kittens."

Juniper turned around slowly and allowed Twig to

leap out of her arms. "I guuuuueeeesss," she pouted, watching him run back under the bench to check on his new brood. "But he's still a genius," she added.

"Agreed," Martin said. "Now what do you say you and I go see if we can't find a bed for these babies that's better than a bunch of old paint rags. There might be a few other things Twig and company will need, too. Like kitten formula and bottles . . ."

"Ooooohhh . . . we can feed them like babies!" Juniper glowed with happiness.

Martin caught his wife's eye as he steered Juniper out of the annex. He had a ton of questions about how and why so many lost animals had appeared in his work area with his middle daughter, but knew it would be easier to let Georgia get to the bottom of it without an Academy Award–winning performance from their youngest distracting them all.

"I just *knew* Twig had a good reason for scaring me like that!" Juniper gushed. "He's very smart, you know. Smarter than any dumb dawwwgg . . ."

Juniper kept on talking, her voice growing more and more faint until finally the annex was silent. For another long moment—at least long to Morgan—nobody spoke. Morgan could feel the weight of the questions everyone wanted to shout at her. And a part of her wanted to shout right back, "We did it! Ember and I did it! We found Twig!" That part felt victorious. She wanted this to be a celebration!

She hazarded a small smile at Forrest, who smiled timidly back. He looked a little scared—the fear, she realized, was for her. The looks on her mom's, Shelby's, and Roxanne's faces were not happy in the least. Even Pedro was frowning.

"So, you decided to take it upon yourself to use one of our training dogs to search for Twig—is that what happened? And then the two of you got locked in?" Georgia asked. "Do you think that was a good idea, mein Schatz?"

Morgan hated when her mom asked the kinds of questions there were no good answers to. And when her German came out because one of them had done something wrong? That was never good. "I'm sorry I worried everyone," Morgan stammered. "It's just, I knew if I had Ember to help me, we could find Twig. And we did—"

"You did," Georgia interrupted in her sternest voice. "But you broke a lot of rules doing it—important rules we have for very important reasons."

Morgan sniffed.

"I know you were only trying to help," Roxanne chimed in. Her light skin shone in the dark barn. She sounded less stern than Morgan's mom, but her words cut deeper. "Ember is at a very fragile stage in her training. Taking commands from multiple sources, searching for animals, and changing targets can confuse or frustrate her. Your adventure might set us back several weeks, unfortunately. It might even prevent Ember from completing her training."

Morgan gulped.

Pedro gave Morgan a sympathetic look but

nodded his agreement. "Even if she gets back on track, she probably won't be ready in time for the handler I had in mind," he said sadly.

Morgan blinked back tears and dropped to her knees to put her arm around Ember.

The Lab had come out from under the bench, where she was watching the nest of kittens when she heard her name. She looked up into the tense, sad faces of the people and wondered what was going on. She'd found what she was looking for and more— why didn't anyone seem happy about it?

Wiggling out from under Morgan's hold, Ember ducked her head to check on the kittens and then came back to sit beside Morgan again. Ember did not like the way the people were talking. Or the way Morgan was getting smaller. But she couldn't stop thinking about the litter under the workbench. After a minute, she crawled back underneath the table and curled her body protectively around Twig and the dozing babies.

Lying with the cats in the darkness reminded her of sleeping with her litter in the dark den under the house that burned. It reminded her of the danger her pack had faced together. She didn't want these tiny cats to be alone in the dark with no one to save them.

"I'm sorry," Morgan said, and meant it. She was sorry she had worried her family, and she was especially sorry that she'd hurt Ember's chances of becoming certified and finding a handler to partner with forever.

"We'll keep working with her," Roxanne said. She would have liked to reassure Morgan that it would all be fine, but she had seen dogs derailed by less.

Morgan could only nod. If she opened her mouth, she was afraid a sob would come out.

"Well, at least we solved the mysteries," Forrest piped up from behind the shelf where he'd been watching everything. He was anxious to change the subject. He hated it when his sisters were in trouble . . . it was almost as bad as being in trouble himself.

"Most of them, anyway," Georgia agreed. "There's just one more thing I can't quite figure out." She cocked her head, raised one eyebrow, and turned to peer at Shelby. Her oldest child was lingering at the edge of one of the tall shelves, inspecting the pink ends of the hair she'd only recently been allowed to straighten, listening to every word and hoping her part in the scheme would go unnoticed. "And that's how *Shelby* knew exactly where to find everyone . . ."

18

Thwack! Morgan was rudely awakened when a pillow landed on her face.

"Hey!" She shoved it aside and rubbed her eyes. When the sleep cleared, her older sister came into view on the other side of the room they shared. Shelby had her arms crossed over her chest and was glowering at her.

"It's time to get up," she grumped.

Morgan yawned and tossed the pillow back. There was really no reason for *her* to get up, but she knew better than to point that out to Shelby.

"I can't believe I have to spend the last weeks of *my* summer vacation doing *your* chores," Shelby complained, pulling off her sleep cap and slipping a lightweight sweatshirt over her head.

Morgan couldn't believe it, either. Her parents had gone heavy on the irony in choosing the sisters' punishments for breaking the rules. Shelby, because she had shown a "lack of responsibility" when she didn't alert her parents to Morgan's reckless behavior, had to take over all the morning kennel cleaning and feeding chores. While Morgan, the reckless one who actually *lived* to clean kennels and feed dogs even when she didn't have to, was not allowed in or around the canine pavilion *at all*. For now.

"There is no way you get to just lie here and snore while I scoop poop," Shelby said. She dabbed on some lip balm and swooped her hair into a ponytail, pulling the pink sections free so they hung next to her face. She checked her appearance in the closet mirror. With her hair back, she looked even more like their mother. "You need to own your part of this mess." She sounded like their mother, too, but when she swallowed, she felt a small lump in her throat—a chunk of guilt. She knew that her punishment was well deserved. And every time she took Ember out for her morning walk, she felt the lump growing. Ember was the one who was really suffering for what she and her sister had done. While it wasn't clear to Shelby what setbacks Ember was experiencing, she had seen Roxanne and Pedro deep in conversation about her, and their looks of concern spoke volumes.

Morgan didn't dare close her eyes again. She threw back the covers and stumbled down the hall toward the bathroom. The good thing about being up needlessly early was that the family bathroom hog was still snoozing.

In the kitchen, Morgan scrambled two eggs, buttered two slices of toast, and put out two plates. She honestly felt bad that Shelby had gotten into trouble for not telling on her, although not as bad as she felt about the possibility that she had messed things up for Ember.

"Is that for me?" Shelby asked, looking shocked when she got back from the pavilion and saw the full plate waiting on the table.

Morgan nodded.

Shelby started to sit down, then sniffed her hand. "Ugh! Dog spit!" She stuck out her tongue and hurried to wash her hands in the kitchen sink.

Morgan hid a smile. If Shelby's hands smelled like spit, she'd obviously let the dogs lick her.

"How are the dogs?" Morgan asked.

Shelby sighed. "They're good. I think they miss you, though."

"And Ember . . . has she . . ." Morgan couldn't quite bring herself to ask what she wanted to know. "Have they . . . ?"

"I don't know," Shelby replied. "I can tell that Pedro and Roxanne are worried about her, but I don't know what decisions have been made. Even Forrest is keeping quiet."

Morgan groaned. Why did her big-mouth brother decide to clam up now?

Shelby looked around the kitchen and leaned closer to Morgan. She wasn't anxious to get in trouble again, and aiding and abetting her sister to get closer to any of the dogs would be bad, but . . . "I think Pedro and Roxanne are going to do some dog and handler introductions this afternoon."

Morgan's heartbeat quickened.

"They're doing the intros on the training ground, after the handler seminar is over. You could probably watch . . . you know, from a distance or under the bleachers or something." Shelby looked around again and took a big bite of breakfast. "I seriously doubt that Ember's going to be one of the dogs they introduce," she said when she'd swallowed, "but I figured you'd want to know either way."

Morgan resisted the urge to hug her sister. "Thanks," she whispered instead.

Shelby gave Morgan a nod, then cocked her head to the side and drew a quick breath. There were noises coming from upstairs, and if she wasn't mistaken, they were the sounds of Juniper leaving the kids' bathroom. "I call next shower!" Shelby yelled before shoving the last of her egg in her mouth and racing for the stairs. She wanted to get the dog hair, drool, and smell off her before she met her friends to go back-to-school shopping . . . it was quite possible that Ryan, the boy from bio, would be in attendance.

🐾 🐾 🐾

Morgan sat on the ground, hidden beneath the bleachers and trying to focus. She'd brought a book with her to make the wait easier, only it *wasn't* making the wait easier. She kept reading the same paragraph over and over because the information seemed to bounce off her brain like a rubber ball, unable to penetrate her thoughts, which were taken up by Ember.

She looked through the narrow slats at the empty training ground for the hundredth time. And then, finally, she saw a dog. Unfortunately, it was not one of the dogs in training, it was just sweet, lumbering Cocoa, followed by her grandma and Forrest. Apparently, Morgan wasn't the only one who wanted to watch the meet and greet.

Introduction day was always fun to observe. Sometimes the connection between a dog and a handler was instantaneous. When that happened, it was almost like watching two cartoon characters fall in love. While nobody's eyes changed to red hearts and big clouds of love didn't magically appear around them, the connection was so obvious, they should have. And even when the bond was a little slower to form, you could usually tell if there was something there.

Other times there was no connection at all. And

some dogs and handlers simply didn't mix. "Oil and water," Frances would say. "It can't be forced."

Morgan shrunk back as Frances and Forrest found seats on the bleachers right above her head. Cocoa put her big brown nose up to the slats and sniffed. She knew Morgan was there, but wouldn't give her away . . . she hoped.

Finally Roxanne appeared, headed for the grounds with three dogs on short leads. Morgan spied Bucko the black Lab, Tucker the border collie mix, and a shepherd named Ava. No Ember.

She knew it was unlikely that Ember would be ready, but she had held out hope nonetheless. Now, racked with guilt, her heart sank.

No Ember. And now she was trapped under the bleachers until the introductions were over—she had no choice but to watch the event that Ember was supposed to be participating in, the event that Ember *would* have been participating in, if it weren't for her.

She slumped back against the wooden structure

and gloomily watched Pedro and the three handlers he'd been working with walk over to greet the dogs. The woman in the group approached the dogs first. She held out her hand, fingers curled under so that they could sniff her, and talked to them in a light voice. Morgan was too far away to make out what she was saying, but could tell she was approaching the dogs appropriately.

It was clear, at least to Morgan, that the woman really liked the shepherd. It must have been clear to Ava, too, because when the woman started to walk away Ava turned herself into a dog pretzel. She flopped onto the handler's feet and rolled onto her back, begging for a belly rub.

The woman laughed but resisted the tempting tummy and stepped back to let the other handlers meet the pups. A lanky blond guy was next. He had a big smile and a friendly way with the dogs. After he greeted Tucker with a pet, the border collie seemed to decide that they were a team. He kept his eyes glued on the guy . . . even when he walked back to stand by Pedro.

The last handler was tall with dark skin, a buzz cut, and broad shoulders. Morgan admired the way he squatted down to greet the dogs, making himself less intimidating. He spoke to and pet each one, letting them get used to him. Morgan squinted through the slats. She did not see any hearts in his eyes.

When every dog had been introduced, Pedro and Roxanne paired dog-and-human teams randomly and had the handlers give some simple instructions to the dogs to see how they did together.

Morgan watched carefully as they ran through the drills. She couldn't see everything she wanted to through the slats, but she saw enough to know after a few circuits that Ava and the woman and Tucker and the blond guy were natural teams. Bucko seemed to do well with the last man, too. The Lab listened to commands and looked to the big guy who'd squatted down to give praise, which Bucko loved. But as Morgan observed them working she sensed that something was off. The man's smile was . . . sad.

It looked like he was holding something back.

19

Marcus Riley looked out over the training field at the Sterling Center. The grass on the field and the low, oak-covered hills beyond was mostly yellow brown this late in the California summer. The summer had been dry, dry, dry, and it was officially fire season soon, though the flames did not go by a calendar. Fire could be touched off anytime in these conditions, and it was making the firefighter extra anxious to get home.

For three weeks, Marcus had been living on the ranch, in the handlers' quarters, taking training

classes from Pedro Sundal. He was here to be part-
nered with a search and rescue dog. The crew at the
fire station where Marcus worked in the mountains
had wanted to add a SAR dog to their team for a
long time and had pressed Marcus into coming to
Sterling. In truth, Marcus had thought it was a good
idea, too. And he loved the class. Pedro was smart,
and funny, and a real dog guy. Just like Marcus. But
now . . .

Running his hand over his close-clipped Afro,
Marcus studied the dogs on the field. They were
alert, intent, attuned. They were all really good dogs
and eager to bond.

It was *Marcus* who was having second thoughts. His
dog, Sadie, whom he'd had since he was a boy, had
been gone only a few months. Sadie's passing was
part of the reason his crew thought Marcus needed a
new companion—why not use this opportunity to get
a SAR dog? He was going to get another dog at some
point, anyway . . . wasn't he?

Watching one of Roxanne's star canines, Bucko, run back across the field with ears and tail flying high and scent cloth caught between his teeth, Marcus felt torn. There was no doubting that Bucko was a good dog—and good at tracking. It was just . . .

"Not him, huh?" Pedro asked when he heard Marcus's heavy sigh. He could see that Marcus was resistant, and Pedro forced back his own disappointment. Barbara and Dylan, the other handlers he'd been working with, had both hit it off immediately with Ava and Tucker. And even though Bucko was an amazing dog who *seemed* like a great match for Marcus—his thick black coat was well suited for the snowy mountains, and his sociable nature was well suited for the firehouse—Pedro knew deep inside that Bucko wasn't Marcus's real match. Ember was. She just wasn't ready.

"You'll feel it. When it's the right dog, you'll know," Pedro said quietly, placing a hand on Marcus's shoulder. In their three weeks together, he'd come to appreciate Marcus's thoughtfulness and subtle sense of humor.

Marcus forced a smile. "That obvious, huh? I mean, I love dogs, and I can't wait to work with one."

"But . . ." Pedro flashed Marcus a genuine smile in return.

"I guess I'm not over my first puppy love." Marcus had told Pedro about losing Sadie when he'd started. The loss of her still felt fresh.

"Give it time," Pedro advised. "Your training doesn't expire, and Bucko here will be a star player on some other team."

Marcus smiled back at the trainer, grateful that Pedro wasn't pushing him. Still, he felt sad and a little deflated as he picked up his water bottle and headed to the handlers' lodge. Without a dog partner, his training here was done. And although he was not looking forward to going home and telling his crew he hadn't brought them the new, four-legged team member they'd been hoping for, he wanted to hit the road as soon as possible and put this failure behind him.

"That's not all the dogs, you know!"

Marcus was so lost in his thoughts he jumped when a girl with dust-covered jeans appeared on the path in front of him from out of nowhere. She was winded and standing right in his way. She swallowed hard.

"Wha-what?" He shook his head as if to clear his vision. When he looked again, the girl was still there. She licked her lips and started talking, fast.

"There's another dog. In the pavilion. She's rescue material. She's got an incredible nose. And she's ready, I promise. If you just come meet her you'll . . . Oh." The girl stopped and stuck out her hand. She was forgetting her manners. "I'm Morgan," she introduced herself. "I live here."

"Marcus." He shook her hand and couldn't help but be amused . . . and a little impressed by the girl's exuberance.

"Great, Marcus. Nice to meet you. So if you'll just come with me to the—"

"Whoa, whoa! Listen, Morgan. It sounds like you've got a great dog. I just don't know." Marcus held up his hands to try to get the girl to slow down. "Maybe I'm the one who's not ready."

Marcus turned and walked to the room where he'd been staying. The girl followed like a shadow, lingering in the doorway while he packed his bag.

"I've got to go now," he said. "I've got a long drive in front of me." He knew he should probably stick around and say goodbye to Pedro and the folks he'd been training with. Right now all he could think about was getting out of there. He'd call from the road.

"Just please come and meet her," the girl pleaded, not giving up as she followed him to his truck. "When you meet her, you'll know."

Marcus shook his head and climbed into the cab of the truck. "Sorry, kid." He pulled the door closed and started the engine. He just barely heard the girl's voice as he pulled out of the lot.

"Ember is perfect for you!"

Marcus turned right out of the parking lot and drew a deep breath. The dog blanket on the seat beside him, the one he had never removed after Sadie died, caught his eye. He hated that empty seat. The empty spot in his chest . . . in his life.

Ember is perfect for you!

That name. It echoed in his head and sparked something. Had the kid really said "Ember"?

At the next intersection, Marcus turned the truck around. When he pulled back into the parking lot, the girl was still standing there. Her head was low and she was staring at her feet, but when she looked up and saw him, a massive smile spread across her face. She was at the truck door before he'd even turned off the engine. Then she was pulling him by the hand. She was a lot stronger than her small frame suggested!

"You won't regret this," she said, pulling him more urgently.

"Listen, no promises," Marcus cautioned her. Resistance was futile. But meeting a dog was not committing to a dog, he told himself.

When they got to the pavilion, Morgan stopped outside the doors. "I can't go in there. I'm, um, kind of grounded, so you're on your own," she explained, feeling a flash of guilt. In spite of everything, this was the right thing to do—she could feel it! "She's halfway down the row of kennels, on the left," she huffed as she practically pushed Marcus into the building. "She's a yellow Lab with big brown eyes. You can't miss her. Her name is Ember."

The door swung shut, and the name echoed again in Marcus's head. *Ember.*

The Lab was asleep on the bed in her kennel when she heard the door. She lifted her head—someone was coming. Her ears pricked up, and she listened to the footfalls, trying to get a whiff of whoever was on their way in. It wasn't Forrest—she knew his smell well. It wasn't Morgan, either. Or Roxanne. Or Pedro, who often smelled like Flamin' Hot Cheetos. Ember stood up and walked to the gate at the front of the kennel. No, it wasn't any of the people she was used to smelling at the ranch, but there was something familiar about the person's smell. She sniffed again and began to wag.

"Ember?" a deep voice asked.

She wagged faster.

"You can't be the same Ember . . ."

A man with a dark face and deep voice crouched down and looked at her closely. He narrowed his sparkly eyes and curled his fingers through the chain link separating them, pressing his face closer. Then he reached up to open the gate. "Can you?"

Ember whirled. She ran the few steps back to her bed to grab her most treasured toy and then spun back around to present it to *this* man. *The* man. She was moving so quickly she nearly bowled him over, and he sat down on the floor, laughing.

Ember dropped her glove in the man's lap, and he picked it up. It was hard to recognize, chewed and torn and slobbered on. But it was also unmistakable.

Marcus stared at the glove and then reached out to pet the glowing yellow dog's scruff. He felt between her shoulder blades and located a small scar with no hair in the shape of a diamond beneath her fur.

Ember barked once. Hello. Again. Then she licked the dimple on Marcus's cheek. He tasted like glove.

Marcus buried his face in the dog's yellow fur. Ember's fur. "Well, I guess you can," he whispered.

20

Ember held on to the whimper in her throat. She didn't let it go, even though it wanted to come out . . . just like *she* wanted to come out of her kennel. She sat on her haunches, watching Pedro and Roxanne. They were looking at something in the book Roxanne was always writing in, their heads close together.

"The disruption in her training can't be ignored," Roxanne said. Her green eyes were full of indecision. "And we haven't had a chance to *really* see if her prey drive will be a problem. There will definitely be things she wants to chase and hunt in the backcountry . . ."

Pedro nodded his understanding. "It's a tough call—maybe the toughest we've ever had to make."

"I'd like another solid month to test her out— maybe more," Roxanne said. "We know she's a dog who needs to work, and if we send her out too early, we might just lose her a job."

Pedro hadn't stopped nodding. "It's one hundred por ciento your call. I have seen them together, and Ember is definitely the dog for Marcus, no question. But if she's not ready, she's not ready. And unfortunately Marcus can only stay three more weeks, tops. They need him back at the station."

Ember cocked her head and tried to hold still. She was ready to get out. To get her vest on. To see her rescuer. To get to work. Marcus had come to see her three days in a row. They went on walks and they played, but they didn't work. She wanted to work.

The whimper escaped, and Roxanne looked over at Ember, as if she would hold the answer. Ember wagged, her slender body full of excitement and hope.

She so wanted to please. And she had done well . . .

"Ember is still occasionally distractible, but I guess no more than before Morgan took her on that little search and rescue mission."

Pedro smirked. "And she did *find* Twig," he added. "Not *hunt* him."

Roxanne sighed. "I know. And things in the Sterling house have settled down significantly since. But while that's a nice benefit, it obviously can't impact this decision." She raised an eyebrow and pointed her chin toward Shelby, who was at the end of the row hosing down dog kennels. She had a bandanna covering her nose, but it didn't hide her scowl.

Pedro chuckled at the sight of the oldest Sterling. "She's doing a good job in spite of herself." His gaze traveled down the row of kennels to where Ember was still sitting, trying hard to be patient. "I know there could be issues with changing who is giving Ember commands, but there's no denying the bond that's already developed between Marcus and Ember—it's one of the strongest I've seen."

"I know," Roxanne agreed. "It's deeper, somehow. She totally lights up when he appears, and that's on top of her usual Ember glow!" She sighed and rubbed her forehead. "Well, you've heard me say more than once that no training is the same and nothing is ever straightforward. So . . . I say let's give it a shot."

Pedro grinned.

Roxanne pulled out her radio and put a call out to Forrest. "You and Morgan can head to your designated places—the training session is a go," she said into the device.

"Awesome!" Forrest replied, and Roxanne could hear Morgan whooping in the background.

Shelby came out of the last kennel that had to be cleaned and re-coiled the hose on the rack on the wall. "Only four more days, and then it's back to having mornings to myself!" she called to everyone happily, pausing at Ember's gate to give the yellow Lab a morning greeting.

Ember wagged her response, licking Shelby's fingers through the fencing in a friendly hello. "Who's a good girl?" Shelby crooned. "Who's the girl who found the missing kitty?" Life had been *so much better* since Twig was located—it was almost worth her dog-care punishment. Almost. "Good luck today," she added in a whisper. She didn't want Roxanne and Pedro to know she'd been listening in.

Shelby was just getting to her feet when Ember's wag triple-timed. "You're happy I'm leaving?" Shelby mock sulked before turning to see Marcus, who was coming through the door. "Ah, I see how it is!" she laughed.

"Morning, everyone!" Marcus's booming voice filled the pavilion, and he looked over at Ember out of the corner of his eye. He wanted to rush over but knew better than to get her excited for play if there was work to be done.

He joined Pedro and Roxanne to find out if today was the day. If they were going to do a trial.

Ember watched, wagging and wagging and wagging. She kept the rest of her body still and didn't bark. She could tell by the smells of the people stealing glances at her that it was the right thing to do. And she didn't have to wait very long for Marcus to come say hello.

"Ready, girl?" he asked as he crouched in front of her kennel holding her vest. "I think it's time."

He opened the door to her kennel, and after giving him a hello lick, Ember stopped wagging and stilled so he could strap on her vest. It felt good to have his strong hands reaching around her and his familiar smell right next to her. It felt right.

Marcus clipped on the lead and they followed Roxanne and Pedro outside. He had to admit he'd been feeling nervous—or his coffee was having a stronger jittery effect than usual—but walking along-side Ember calmed him. He didn't have to do this alone, and neither did she. They would do it together.

"Forrest and Morgan have had plenty of time to get to their hiding places," Roxanne said when they reached the training starting point. "Pedro and I are going to head into the trailer here, and you two can start. Keep her on the lead so she doesn't get too far ahead. Once Ember is on the trail, we'll follow at a good distance—we want it to be clear to her that you are in charge . . ." She reached an arm out to Marcus. "Try to relax. It's a big day for both of you, but it's also just the first session. Try not to give her any acci-dental signals, and try not to worry!"

Marcus exhaled slowly. Roxanne had experience reading people as well as dogs! "Thanks." He watched Roxanne and Pedro head to the trailer and close the door.

"It's you and me now, Em," he said. He reached into his pocket for the sock Roxanne had given him.

"You, me, and a not-too-smelly sock." He held it out to her, and she buried her nose in it, taking her time. There was no scent pad. There were no treats. The sock was it. Finally, she pulled away.

Ember looked up at him, her brown eyes glowing with anticipation. Marcus could tell she was working hard to hold still. She was really just a puppy! He took a deep breath and reminded himself that his job was to give commands and remain neutral . . . let Ember do the work. "Just another training session," he murmured to himself. "But one we definitely want to get right." He gave Ember a steady look, trying to convey the importance of their mission with his eyes. This wasn't playtime. This was serious. They had to show potential if they were going to be matched. "Find!" he said in his booming voice.

Ember understood. She turned away from him and put her nose to the ground, sniffing this way and then that way, zigzagging over the dry earth. She stopped for a moment, sniffing more intently. She'd found the start of her trail, and she was off. Marcus watched, impressed by her focus, and then realized with a jolt that he had to follow! He started to move after her just in time to avoid getting his arm yanked.

Marcus trailed as far back as the lead would allow. It was just a precaution, and he knew better than to stay too close. In the field, he wouldn't use a lead. Ember would bark an alert when she found what—or whom—she was looking for, and bark again if he took a long time to reach her side.

"Just a training session," he murmured to himself. "No pressure. We got this."

Ember sniffed the air, the trail, the air again. She had picked up Forrest's familiar scent quickly—after months of training, it was almost as recognizable to her as the glove's. The boy smell was strong by the second shade structure, weaker toward the plane wreck. A steady scent stream, steadier than the rest, reached her nose. It was coming from the hill up ahead! Ember started in that direction, and then something else caught her nose. A second smell she recognized . . . and hadn't smelled this strongly in a while. She longed to fill her snout with it!

Ember changed course and picked up her pace. She could hear Marcus behind her, working hard to keep up. Soon she was at the rubble pile—the giant pile of stuff where Roxanne taught her to test her steps and trust her feet—where terrain was unsteady. The smell seemed to be gone, though. She raised her nose. Paused. Then she caught it again.

Ember walked along a two-by-four, balancing like a gymnast on a beam, and nosed into an opening. There was the person she'd been smelling and wanting to see: Morgan!

Morgan's stomach clenched, and she dared not breathe. She'd heard Ember coming and willed her to go in another direction. It obviously hadn't worked! She was thrilled that Roxanne had asked her to help with the training test (and wondered if she had purposely forgotten that Morgan wasn't supposed to have dog contact *just* yet), but now it seemed like everything—maybe even introducing Ember to Marcus—had backfired.

Morgan bit her lip. She watched Ember's nose appear . . . and then disappear. She could barely breathe. If Ember barked an alert, it would be a "fail"—proof that she was still too distractible. Now, and maybe forever.

She exhaled silently. She couldn't make a peep! The brown tip of Ember's nose poked through an opening above her head again, closer this time. Her damp, soft nostrils twitched. Morgan closed her eyes and waited. At last she heard Ember's paws moving away down the piece of lumber . . . she was leaving. Morgan exhaled again, loudly this time. Ember had not alerted on the wrong person. She was back on the trail.

Morgan adjusted her body position. She'd been holding herself so rigidly that her left foot was asleep. She had to stay here until the exercise was over, and after stretching a little, she resettled. Several minutes later, she heard Ember's clear barks . . . the signal that she'd found Forrest. Grinning, Morgan sat up and threw aside the rubble over her head, feeling as victorious as the yellow Lab. "Yes!" she shouted with her arms in the air.

21

Marcus pushed back his covers, sat up, and put his feet on the smooth wooden floor in the dorm-like room of the handlers' lodge. It was week three of training with Ember, and he still couldn't believe how happy she made him . . . how happy working with her made him. All of his uncertainty and confusion about handling a SAR dog had vanished. His precious Sadie would always have a place in his heart—a big place. But actually working with a dog was fulfilling in a way that playing with and loving a dog wasn't. It was just . . . different. It gave them a common goal—something to work toward together—and he suspected it meant as much to Ember.

Pedro told Marcus that Ember was lucky he'd found her, but Marcus knew the luck was his. What were the chances that the tiny puppy he'd rescued from beneath a burning house nearly a year and a half earlier would be a SAR dog in training at Sterling Ranch? It was almost too perfect to be true.

Marcus tied his boots and went out to the common kitchen in the lodge. After pouring himself a cup of coffee, he sat down to breakfast with Pedro and the other handlers. There were four trainees on the ranch right now. Three were taking the initial course to learn to work with dogs, the one he took before he met Ember. There was also Barbara, who had taken the course with him and met her match in Ava, the same day Morgan led Marcus to Ember. Dylan, the man who'd been working with Tucker, hadn't worked out, which, according to Pedro, happened on occasion. It wasn't over, though—Dylan would be back in the spring to try to match with another dog, and Tucker would remain on the ranch until he found the right handler.

Barbara was engrossed in conversation with Pedro, and it was clear that she was worried. Her training session with Ava the day before hadn't gone well—Ava had basically taken off when given the "find" command, and it had taken almost fifteen minutes to locate her. Marcus sensed that the other, newer handlers were worried as well . . . they'd already seen Dylan leave the ranch, and every one of them wanted to succeed.

"You'll get there," Pedro assured Barbara. "There's no perfect recipe . . . it's a process, and every team has bad days. Ava is responding well to you overall, and you both want to get it right. That's the most important thing—you've got the same goal."

Marcus spooned granola and yogurt into his mouth and crunched, feeling comforted by Pedro's words. Training with Ember had gone well—they'd only had a few missteps—but things weren't perfect. Just yesterday Roxanne had stopped him on his way back to the pavilion after their training session.

"Are you picking up on Ember's devotion to you?" she'd asked. "It's highly developed for a dog you've just met. I've never actually seen it so intense before."

Marcus had swallowed hard. "Well, Ember and I didn't exactly just meet."

Roxanne had stopped then and turned to face him, her surprise obvious. "What?"

Marcus had felt like a little kid who'd been caught cheating, and his cheeks grew warm. "I'm certain she's one of the puppies I rescued from a house fire a year or so ago . . . she was the last one and she blacked out from the smoke. I resuscitated her. I'm the one who gave her that mangled glove she loves so much. It was mine . . ." He'd trailed off, wondering why he hadn't thought to tell Roxanne and Pedro this before. Now that they were discussing it, he felt foolish, because it obviously mattered. He hoped he hadn't messed things up. He had nothing but respect for *all* the people who worked at the Sterling Center, and the last thing he wanted was to undermine their work.

Roxanne's reddish eyebrows had risen high above her intense green eyes. "I see," she'd said. "Well, that certainly explains it. I have to be frank with you, Marcus. It would have been better if you had told us this up front. It's not a small development, especially given that she is only borderline ready to be paired with a handler. Devotion creates a whole new set of potential issues. This is crucial information . . . information we should have known."

A lump formed in Marcus's throat. He knew that Roxanne was right, and that he had made a critical mistake. "I realize that now," he'd replied. "It was very clearly my mistake, and I apologize."

That had been the end of the conversation, and they'd walked back to the pavilion with Ember in silence. Now, as Marcus sipped his coffee and scraped up the last few bites in his bowl, he felt worry creeping up on him again. He was eager to address the issue with Pedro and waited patiently for him to finish his conversation with Barbara. At last, Barbara excused herself and Marcus turned to speak. Pedro beat him to it.

"Roxanne told me that you and Ember have a history . . ." he began. "So, why didn't you tell us?"

Marcus felt his face warm with embarrassment all over again. "To be honest, I didn't really think about it," he admitted. "It sounds pretty stupid when I say it now, but it's true. I didn't think it would matter. It seemed like a good thing, you know, like it would help us bond."

Pedro's voice was cautious. "Based on the fact that you rescued and resuscitated her, Ember probably thinks of you as her hero—her savior, even. That can really complicate things. If she puts you above everything else, it can get in the way of the work that needs to be done. Victims have to come first on a rescue."

Marcus stared into his mug of coffee. He knew that *now*.

"We understand that this was an honest mistake, and a pretty amazing coincidence!" Pedro said, his expression lightening. "Not many people would choose to resuscitate a dog, or would even know how. Thanks for saving her."

Marcus exhaled. He had saved her, and it was worth it. It was the future he was concerned about.

"We're not going to change course, but you need to know that your history will have an impact. It's going to be up to you to be on the watch for changes in her behavior when you are training and working, and to make adjustments as best you can," Pedro said.

Marcus nodded, relieved. "Yes. Okay," he said. He understood from experience what Roxanne and Pedro were saying. The trauma he and Ember experienced when they first met bound them together, which was good. It also complicated their relationship, which was bad.

Maybe finding Ember again really *was* too good to be true.

Pedro clapped a hand on Marcus's shoulder, then stood up to clear his breakfast dishes. "Now that we've addressed it, let's focus on moving forward. You and Ember are making solid progress. We all want to see you become the best team you can be."

Marcus nodded, impressed with Pedro's honest and forgiving approach. They cleared their plates, and Pedro headed to the pavilion to get ready for his morning sessions. Marcus had most of the day to wait, so he went up to his room to read up on SAR scenarios and rescue gear. He was familiar with many of the items a handler would carry into the backcountry on a rescue, but the list was long, and with the added responsibility of caring for Ember, there were items to add. He needed to do more research.

Finally, in the late afternoon, it was time to head

to the kennels. When he arrived, Morgan was there feeding and cleaning up after the dogs, and she greeted him with a broad smile. She was obviously thrilled to be allowed back in the pavilion. And the dogs seemed thrilled, too.

"You're really great with the dogs," Marcus complimented her.

Morgan looked up, but the dog she was leashing continued to gaze at her adoringly, oblivious to the other people in the pavilion.

"See? You're not the only one around here to be worshipped by a dog," Pedro joked, overhearing their conversation and walking over to join them. "Only with Morgan, it's *every* dog. I mean, I like to think we're all good with them, but Morgan is our resident animal whisperer."

Marcus nodded his agreement. "I can see that. And I can see why."

Morgan lit up at the compliment, then got embarrassed and turned away.

"And Pedro is our human whisperer," Roxanne added as she joined the group, carrying the morning's stack of training logs under one arm and a tangle of leads and scent articles in the other. She also had a sample backpack of SAR equipment slung over her shoulder. "And do we ever need him!" She shifted the logs under her arm. "Let me put these things away and we can get you started, okay?"

Marcus nodded. He bent down to pet the dog in the kennel next to him. He felt a bit sheepish knowing that his training had presented its challenges, and a bit nervous. If he and Ember didn't demonstrate that they could work well together, he would have to leave without her. Just the thought made his breathing shallow. They had to be together. They both needed this job! Marcus forced himself to take a deep breath and stand back up. When he straightened, Roxanne and Pedro were ready for their session.

"Oscar and Eloise left to hide in their respective

places early this morning, so both of their trails will be old enough to be a real challenge," Roxanne explained. "This will be a good test of Ember's—and your—progress. She should be tracking Eloise . . . Oscar is the decoy. Marcus hadn't met Oscar, but Eloise had come to dinner in the handlers' lodge the previous week. She lived in town and was a part-time employee of the Sterlings. It was obvious that she loved dogs, and Pedro had explained that she was *also* exceptionally patient, so she was often the victim when a dog neared certification. Eloise had also just applied to be a trainer. Oscar, from what Marcus had been told, was new in town but had a lot of experience with dogs.

"You'll be on your own out there today," Pedro added. "Roxanne and I will wait in the observation trailer and keep track of time."

Roxanne handed Marcus a walkie-talkie. "We will be able to hear you through this, and will come out when Eloise has been found . . ." She trailed off, nodding toward Morgan. "And I suspect there will be others joining you after the search as well."

Morgan turned to Roxanne, her eyes alight. "It's okay for me to go out to the victim? I mean, after Ember finds her?"

Roxanne nodded. "Of course. You and Forrest have been a huge help in training Ember. You should participate in her successes . . . and failures."

Morgan didn't waste a second. She set the last fresh water bowl inside a kennel, wiped her hands on her shorts, and dashed out of the pavilion. "I'm going to go find Forrest and tell him . . . we'll meet you at the trailer!" she shouted as she ran.

Though Morgan seemed to miss the word "failures," Marcus didn't. He took a deep breath and tried to ignore his nervousness as he pulled Ember's lead and vest off their hook and walked to her kennel. His heart lifted at the sight of her, like always. No matter what anyone said, he knew deep inside that they were something special together. He just hoped they could be successful as a SAR team . . . that finding her again and having the chance to work together wasn't too good to become a reality.

Ember let out a happy bark and wagged like mad when she saw Marcus coming to open her cage. She retrieved her beloved, chewed-up glove and dropped it at his feet. As soon as Marcus clipped on her lead and her vest, though, her demeanor changed. It was time to get to work. When Marcus stood, she stood, waiting patiently by his side until it was time for him to lead her out to the training grounds.

Roxanne and Pedro walked behind the pair, chatting until they got themselves settled in the observation trailer.

While Marcus waited for the signal that he could begin the search, the youngest Sterling kid—Juniper—walked by with the cat called Twig. Marcus hadn't had a ton of interaction with either Juniper or Twig, though he'd heard the story of the cat going missing and adopting an abandoned litter of kittens. And Ember being the one to locate them. He could tell from their brief interactions that Twig had a thing for Ember . . . and that the feeling was mutual. Ember's attention zeroed in on the cat in a flash.

"Stop wiggling, Twig!" Juniper demanded.

Marcus felt Ember start to step forward, then correct herself and stand steady at his side.

For her part, Juniper was not letting the cat go. Marcus had to admire her ability to hold a rather large, determined-to-escape, squirming cat. "Don't even look at that dog, Twiggy," she said. "We've got much more important things to attend to . . . kittens!" She marched off, holding the cat so tightly Marcus half wondered if the tabby could breathe.

When they were gone, Marcus looked down at Ember, proud of her restraint. "Good girl." He gave her a quick pat and unclipped her lead. Her priorities were in the right place. It was like she knew that they had to prove themselves, too. Their future together depended on it.

The walkie-talkie crackled, giving Marcus the all clear to begin. Still he waited another few minutes, getting himself centered. He didn't want to pass on any anxiety to Ember. When he felt a sense of calm in both of them, he held out Ember's scent article— Eloise's T-shirt.

Ember stepped forward and took a whiff. This smell was new to her, and she stepped back and then forward again, this time inhaling more deeply. Marcus had been surprised to learn that dogs inhaled scent in many different ways . . . sometimes casually, some- times intently, sometimes quickly, and sometimes slowly. But whenever Ember was done, she looked up at Marcus to let him know she was ready, and today was no exception.

Marcus held her gaze for several seconds, trying to silently communicate his desire for her best effort and his commitment to the same himself. Finally he spoke the command. "Find!"

Ember didn't hesitate. She started off toward the plane wreck—the mock crash site set in the hills well beyond the ranch's buildings. She moved in her usual zigzag pattern, finding the places where the smell was strong and where it faded . . . homing in. When Marcus got too far behind, she circled back to him to make sure he was coming. She didn't like getting too far ahead, even though it was her job to be out in front, to scent everywhere.

"I'm here . . . find!" he called. He knew he wasn't supposed to talk to Ember—he was just supposed to let her work. Keeping neutral and quiet was a lot harder than it sounded!

Beyond the mini forest, Ember raised her snout in the air and then dropped her nose even closer to the ground. The trail was right there. Without turning or hesitating, she moved farther up the hill and into some scrub trees. She was close!

Behind her in an open field, Marcus knew Ember was on the right trail even though he couldn't see her. The fact that she hadn't circled back to him was good . . . very good. It showed that she was thinking and acting independently, like a SAR dog, and was not overly focused on—or devoted to—him.

Marcus smiled, realizing that he wasn't nervous anymore, that his nervousness had been replaced with excitement. They were doing it!

Ten minutes later, he heard Ember bark . . . once, twice, three times. And then again, three times more. As a backcountry fireman, Marcus had a lot of experience locating sound in open spaces, and he used that skill now to move toward the noise. When he finally caught up to Ember she was sitting patiently next to Eloise, who was lying perfectly still on the ground as if unconscious. Ember had found her! They had found her!

Marcus approached and clipped on her lead. "Good girl," he said. He gave her a treat, but she was happiest to be pet and praised.

"All clear to get up," he told Eloise, who sat up with a smile and pulled the dead leaves from her light brown hair. She reached a friendly arm up to pet Ember.

"She's got talent," Eloise remarked.

Ember let out a bark of agreement, and Marcus and Eloise laughed. They were chatting about other dogs Eloise had been "rescued" by, when the rest of the training crew approached, Forrest and Morgan at the head of the pack whooping and hollering.

"You did it!" Forrest yelped, giving Ember a good rub behind the shoulders. Morgan pressed her forehead to Ember's. "Such a good dog," she told her softly.

Roxanne waved the stopwatch in her hand, smiling. "Eighteen minutes," she said. "Impressive!"

Pedro clasped Marcus on the back. "Well done," he said.

Marcus exhaled his relief. "I didn't see any signs of her worrying about me," he said. "She circled back once, but she was clear about doing her work. She wasn't too tethered."

Pedro nodded. "Excellent. That doesn't mean it won't come up in the future, but it's a great sign that she understands her job."

Ember let out a happy bark and turned in a circle, chasing her tail. Being surrounded by so many happy people was making her frisky. She barked again, inviting them to join her. The yellow dog loved to work *and* play!

22

Ember's tail was high as Marcus led her out of the pavilion, through the training grounds, and past the building where Marcus slept. But as they walked through the door to the welcome center—the place where she first arrived at Sterling—her golden flag began to droop. It was leaving day. Ember could always sense a goodbye, and she didn't like them. The days before had been filled with her favorite thing: working with Marcus. And there had been a ceremony where Marcus wore his uniform, and they got a piece of paper from Roxanne and Pedro, and everyone from the ranch was there . . . and happy.

She turned back to the door and watched as a small herd of people came through. First came Pedro and Roxanne. Then Morgan and Forrest, who had given her extra kibble this morning. Ember's tail drooped even lower.

The ranch people were still happy, like the day Ember and Marcus had been certified. But there was also a sadness hovering all around them, and it reminded Ember of smelling a ball that she couldn't reach. It was the feeling of loss.

Forrest was the first to crouch by her side. "We're going to miss you, girl," he said, burying his face in her neck. He smelled like dirt and peanut butter and sad. "All of us."

Ember licked his face to tell him she was sad, too, and she would miss him, too. Then Morgan was there, and Shelby. They crowded around her with pets and croons. Ember wagged and licked them all.

"You did so good," Morgan whispered. "I know you're going to be great at this."

"Oh good, we made it!" Juniper burst into the welcome center carrying not one cat, but two!

Ember's tail perked up.

Twig was so busy licking the second small gray ball of fur in Juniper's clutches he forgot to squirm in Juniper's grasp. The ball of fur—the runt of the litter—didn't seem to mind being carried *or* groomed to death.

"Excuse me! Clear the way! It's not easy carrying two cats, you know!" Juniper complained, though she was smiling broadly. She pushed her way past the crowd and up to Ember with cats in arm, barely slowing down. Shelby and Morgan exchanged a laughing look.

"Come on through, Juniper," Forrest teased. He tweaked one of her braids.

"Thanks!" Juniper replied, oblivious to her siblings' teasing.

Ember stepped forward and put her wet nose right

into the tiny kitten's fur, sniffing her small gray head. Twig stared intently at the pair before reaching out a paw and gently putting it on Ember's snout . . . claws in. No scratching.

"I think Twig's gonna miss her!" Forrest said, shaking his head in disbelief. He'd thought the dog and cat were a mismatched pair, but maybe they were actually pals. He laughed and stroked Ember's golden fur one last time.

Ember's long pink tongue circled up to lap the orange paw on her snout, which Twig didn't seem to mind.

"I guess you're not such a menace," Juniper told Ember. "Twig here is an excellent judge of character." She paused, sizing Ember up anew. "But you're still a *dog*," she said with a sniff.

Everyone laughed at that, and Juniper stepped back, her arms still overloaded with cat.

"Impressive, June Bug," Martin said. He and Georgia had come to say goodbye, too, and they were watching their youngest, awaiting disaster. "Those cats really trust you," he added.

Ember gave a lick to Martin and Georgia, and then the lady who was always with Cocoa. Cocoa, for her part, offered a slow wag and a friendly parting sniff.

Roxanne and Pedro came last and got good long nuzzles. By the end Ember's ears were drooping . . . goodbyes made her think of old times, hard times.

Roxanne shook Marcus's hand. "Congratulations again on your certification. You earned it. I hope we didn't rush things. You two may still have some details to work out, but I think you're going to make a great team. I think you *are* a great team."

Marcus held out a hand, but Roxanne ignored it, hugging him instead. "Hope you don't mind. I'm a hugger. And now we're family." She grinned and squatted down to talk to Ember.

"You're going to do great," she said. "You're ready for the field, and you're in excellent hands. Marcus will take good care of you."

Marcus! Ember's ears perked up and her wag returned. Yes, she loved Marcus. Marcus saved her. Marcus worked with her. Marcus gave her . . .

"Oh, wait! We almost forgot!" Morgan dashed out of the welcome center and returned with the best-smelling thing in Ember's world. "Here you go, Em."

Ember took her glove in her mouth and carried it out to Marcus's truck. When she was settled in the passenger seat, Marcus climbed in behind the wheel. He glanced over. It was great to have a copilot again. The empty spot was filled with the warmth of an Ember.

"Reach out anytime with questions or concerns," Pedro said through the open window. "We're here to help."

"I can't thank you enough . . . for everything," Marcus said gratefully. "My time here has been wonderful, and well spent."

Pedro's handshake was firm and friendly. "Our pleasure, Marcus. De verdad," he added, because it was the truth. "Take care of each other out there."

With a final wave, Marcus put the truck in reverse. Ember sniffed the air. Marcus smelled like happy and sad and smoke . . . and home. He ruffled the fur on Ember's head. "You're going to like the station," he told her. "And my place, too. I mean, our place. I mean, your new home." Ember wagged. She had Marcus and her glove . . . As far as she was concerned she was home already.

🐾 🐾 🐾

Life in Big Fork was good. There was space to run and roam, and a lot of trees. And rivers and lakes and even more trees.

"Come on, girl . . . I've got to get to the station," Marcus called. They'd just finished a training session with Victor, whom she'd had to find. Victor was tall and skinny and smelled like coffee and cats. He came with her and Marcus to the open space in the mountains near Marcus's house where they practiced a lot—they both wanted to keep their skills sharp. Sometimes Ember had to find Victor, and sometimes

Victor and Marcus would walk together while Ember found Greta, who also worked at the fire station.

"Ember!" Marcus called a second time . . . something he rarely had to do. Ember was taking her time breathing in all the smells on the way back to the truck. They were different from the smells on the ranch—piney and earthy at the same time—and she was still getting familiar with them.

Ember hopped into the truck and settled between Marcus and Victor. She liked going to the station— the firefighters were nice to her, and there were usually treats. The only problem was that Ember didn't get to go along with Marcus on the calls. Dogs didn't fight fires . . . only people did that. When Marcus was gone, there wasn't much to do other than investigate the station smells and chase mice. Which was fun, but wasn't *work*. Not real work, anyway.

Ember and Marcus had training sessions almost every day, but they didn't last long, and that wasn't real work, either.

"I thought for sure we would have gotten a search call by now." Victor put his hand on Ember's back. He was a big fan of the yellow Lab. And as much as he did not want to pray for disaster, he was anxious to see her in the field . . . for real. When a backcountry rescue call came in, he would go with them.

"Me, too," Marcus said, nodding. "I can't wait for Ember to show her stuff. And I worry she's getting bored with just practice."

"I can relate to that!" Victor replied, his blue eyes crinkling at the corners. "I never know what to do with my time off . . ."

It was a short drive to the station, and soon Ember was hopping down and trotting inside. Marcus unclipped her vest and hung it on her hook on the wall with her leads, next to the row of the squad's fire protection suits. Ember greeted the firefighters with sniffs and wags, and Greta unwrapped a beef bone and offered it to her.

Ember took the bone in her mouth and carried it to

her bed, turning three times before settling. She gave it a few licks and nudged it aside in favor of her favorite treat. The bone was tasty, but it wasn't her glove.

Ember had just gotten her glove nicely covered in slobber when the bell rang, signaling a call. She was on her feet and next to her hook, awaiting her vest before the bell stopped ringing. Marcus was on her heels.

"Standard fire call, Ember," he said as he pulled on his heavy, fire-retardant pants and then the jacket. "You've got to stay here." He pointed her back to her bed and glove. Ember held back a whimper. She understood that dogs didn't fight fires. Still, she wanted to help.

"I know, girl. Our time will come . . . we just have to be patient." Marcus grabbed a helmet. "Be good." Ember rested her chin on her paws and listened as Marcus and the crew climbed into the big truck without her. She swallowed another whimper and licked her glove. It didn't really help. Not much.

When she opened her eyes several hours later, it

was dark outside, and her nose quivered. Smoke. It smelled like smoke. Her ears went flat, and she felt a moment of panic before she remembered where she was . . . at the station. And then Marcus was there.

"I'm back, girl," he said, stroking her scar. The smell of smoke was strong on him. Smoke and sweat and exhaustion. He put his dark head to hers. "I'm back and everything is all right."

Ember licked his hand even though it tasted like soot. She didn't like that Marcus had to fight fires. He always smelled terrible when he came back, and sometimes the smell was so strong it made her want to bury her nose in her bed, or anywhere that didn't smell like smoke. She hated fire. Fire burned. Fire moved and sparked and flared. You couldn't trust it.

Ember licked Marcus's smoky hand again. She trusted him, but she would never trust fire.

Not ever.

23

"Ember, girl . . . it's time," a voice said. Marcus. It was Marcus. Ember lifted her sleepy head and saw his broad shape in the dim light. He was standing over her bed holding her vest. She cocked her head. It was a strange time to train.

"This is it, girl. We got a search call," he said in his deep voice. Ember didn't understand his words, but she understood the vest in his hands. She got to her feet and bowed low in a stretch. Then she stood and let him buckle on her work uniform. The weight of it was a familiar comfort.

In the kitchen, Marcus filled her bowl and packed more of the dry kibble into a bag, along with treats and water. Then he got on the phone. Ember could tell by his voice that this wasn't training. Something serious was happening.

"Okay . . . Okay," Marcus repeated. It was good to hear a familiar voice on the other end of the line. Greta was the incident commander on the mission—the person responsible for everyone on the search. She had already established a base camp and staffed it, as well as a command post for the mission leaders. Only a few designated people would communicate directly with Greta—the team leaders—and Marcus was one of those people.

"Travis and his two daughters have been missing for over twenty-four hours. They were supposed to return from their backpacking trip last night but didn't." Greta supplied the details she had. "The girls are six and eight. I have a team handling confinement to keep the search area from getting any larger, and two more teams coming in from the other side of the pass. I want your team to go directly to the campsite—their last known position. Hopefully Ember can track them from there. I'll send the GPS coordinates. Marcus, be careful. And good luck."

Marcus could hear a touch of nervousness, or maybe adrenaline, in Greta's voice. There was no doubt she could handle being incident commander— she'd taken classes, been on several missions, and shadowed more experienced ICs. Still, this was the first time she'd be fully in charge, and the first time Marcus had gone out with his own dog. It was new territory for both of them.

Marcus reached down and pet Ember behind her ears. She gazed up expectantly, and he couldn't help but smile. Ember wasn't nervous. She couldn't wait to do what she'd been trained to do.

Marcus grabbed the pack and plastic bin he'd

been keeping at the ready since he'd come back from training at Sterling—the one with headlamps and batteries and plastic blankets and water bottles and rope and tools and other things they might need in the field. He added the food bags, filled the water bottles with fresh water, and strapped some hiking poles to the outside of the pack. "Ready, girl?" he asked, slinging the heavy pack over his shoulder.

Ember could tell by Marcus's tone that something was different. Someone was in trouble. She could tell she'd have to do her best. She was ready.

Oh. So. Ready.

Outside, the air was chilly and the sky still dotted with blinking stars. The moon was just a sliver, a curving slice of white glowing in the dark sky. The sun wouldn't be up for several hours, and Marcus turned his headlights on bright as he pulled onto the country highway.

They swung by to pick up Victor, and Ember moved over to make room.

"Game on," Victor said as he climbed into the truck. He still smelled like sleep.

"Looks like," Marcus said. He repeated the information he'd gotten from Greta. "Their car is parked in the Granite Lake trailhead lot, a silver Toyota Highlander."

"Got it." Victor nodded.

The drive to the trailhead was about an hour, but none of them could settle. Ember panted over her handler's lap, and Victor kept changing the radio station, looking for something that would distract them. When they pulled into the trailhead parking lot, it was still dark, and only one car was parked at the far end . . . a silver Highlander.

"We're definitely in the right place," Marcus said as he slid the truck next to the Highlander and swung open his door. "Incident Command is sending other crews from the opposite side, closer to base camp and the search area. We're a little farther out, but Ember needs a scent article to track, so we need to find the campsite, start there." Ember hopped out after him and waited for Marcus and Victor to get their gear situated.

"It's chilly up here," Victor said, pulling another layer out of his pack. "I can see why there's only one car . . . it's pretty late in the season for camping."

"They're closing this trailhead for the winter in a few weeks," Marcus said as he pulled the drawstring on the top of his pack closed and buckled the flap. He shivered slightly and hoisted the pack squarely onto his back, cinching the waist strap. He checked Ember's vest, making sure it was snug and secure before strapping a headlamp on her head. Marcus touched it, and it made a clicking noise. Suddenly she could see the ground in front of her like the sun was up! This was brighter than the lights she'd trained with—it helped her see much farther.

Marcus was in charge for the first part of the journey. He knew the way, and they didn't have anything for Ember to scent with . . . not yet. He held his communication device in one hand and a big piece of paper with all kinds of lines on it in the other.

"I don't know why you still use the paper map when you've got a GPS with a topo map and position accuracy to three meters," Victor said teasingly. "It's so old-school."

"Hey, if my GPS craps out on me, I'll still know where I am and what's around me . . ." Marcus said. "It's a precaution. Besides, I like maps."

Victor shook his head in bemusement. "I get *having* the map with you . . . I don't get the actual carrying it in your hand."

Marcus shrugged. "Blame my grandfather," he said. "The man was serious about map and compass skills."

Ember shook her head lightly to get used to the feel of the light. She trotted along with Marcus and Victor, waiting for a command. The air smelled of pinesap, and earth, and the ground under her paws was cold but also soft with pine needles. All three of the searchers were filled with anxious anticipation.

The campsite was a little over a mile and a half from the parking lot, and they arrived just before dawn. Ember sniffed her way around the site as the sky began to lighten. She didn't find any food scraps . . . just the scent of many small animals, a small soft house full of human smells, and a cold stove. Marcus got on his black box, which crackled loudly in the stillness of the forest.

"We've located the campsite. It's tidy—no signs of distress or hurried departure. I'll update you once we get a scent and we're on the trail," Marcus alerted IC. He switched off the black box and crawled head-first into the tent.

From the outside, Ember noticed that the walls of the soft house moved. She sniffed around the out-side. Dirt. Human sweat. Toothpaste . . .

When Marcus reappeared, he was holding a stiff,

dirty sock speckled with bits of dead leaves and pine needles. It was small, with rainbow stripes—probably belonged to one of the girls. Marcus blew out his breath. He hoped, wherever they were, they were warm and safe.

Marcus held the sock out, and Ember trotted forward to snuffle it in. The smell was fresh. She blew it out and inhaled again, trapping tiny particles in her nose. When the scent was well established, she stepped away from Marcus and sat on her haunches, looking up at him. He looked right back, his eyes serious. Determined. The anxious smell he'd had before was gone. Ember stayed still while he removed her headlight—the sun was on the horizon—and then waited for the command. Finally, it came.

"Find!"

24

Ember began the search right where she was . . . in the campsite. The sock scent was all over. She needed to find where it left the clearing . . . where it trailed off in a specific direction. She smelled around the base of trees and near the smoky fire ring. Then she went back to the soft den. The house with the moving walls was full of intense smells. Ember's nose quivered wildly as she circled the structure again, focusing on the smell of the sock. She widened her circle, spiraling away, nose high, then low, following where the smell led her.

The sunlight hadn't yet cleared the ridge to the east, so the air and the ground were still cold. Ember's breath steamed in front of her as she sniffed her way up the trail excitedly. Victor and Marcus brought up the rear. She was in charge now!

On the other side of a stream, she paused to listen for the men. It was hard to be patient! Humans were slow, and out here in the forest they seemed even slower.

"Good girl, Ember," Marcus said, coming up behind her a little out of breath. He could see impatience in her body language. He could tell she was holding back, for him. "Keep going," he encouraged her, careful not to repeat the command and inadvertently send her on a different trail—searching for whatever she'd scented last.

Ember picked up her pace a little bit, traveling more quickly toward the ridge ahead, easily scrambling over a pile of boulders that had fallen and collected over many years. With her four long legs, she could leap from one to the next, but Marcus and Victor had a harder time navigating the uneven terrain. Victor's long legs helped a little. Looking back, Ember saw he was closer than Marcus.

"I feel like molasses," Marcus grunted in frustration as he pulled himself onto a large, flat, car-sized rock next to Victor. "Heavy molasses!"

"Oh, to be a dog!" Victor said, wiping his brow. The sun was higher now, and the chill in the air was long gone. "Relatively speaking, our legs are pathetic."

"So true," Marcus replied. "And so inconvenient." He looked up at Ember, who was several vertical feet above them and not even panting. "I guess that's why search dogs are so valuable . . . they can cover the terrain of thirty human searchers."

Ember was off again. The top of the scree of rocks was in view, and above that a patch of trees that gave way to a slide of solid granite near the top of a ridge. Marcus wished he knew the area better—he'd never been here before, and a map—paper or electronic— could only tell a person so much. The ridge looked like the top of the mountain from here, but he suspected there were other ridges beyond it that they couldn't see. The Sierra Nevada range was no joke.

It took two hours to get to the top of the scree, where they came across a small lake. Marcus and Victor chugged from their water bottles while Ember lapped at the shore. Marcus got out the canvas travel bowl and filled it with kibble, then offered some GORP to Victor.

"Good old raisins and peanuts! Breakfast of champions," Victor said, taking a large handful. The threesome perched by the shore and filled their bellies, each of them anxious to keep moving and thinking of the unknown paths ahead and the unknown fates of the hikers.

"More?" Marcus asked, holding out the bag. Victor raised a hand. "I'm all GORPed up." Marcus repacked the snack and secured his pack. He radioed base camp to report.

"We're heading up Tabletop Ridge," Marcus said.

"Excellent," Greta replied. "The two other teams we've deployed haven't found anything yet, but they're covering some solid ground."

"I will keep you updated," Marcus said. "Ember's definitely on a trail now." He switched off the radio and holstered it. What they would find at the end of that trail, nobody knew.

Before settling his pack on his back, Marcus pulled out the sock for Ember. She inhaled deeply, paused, and took off at a quick trot. She didn't need the reminder.

The threesome moved forward, with Ember once again ranging far ahead. Marcus was relieved to realize that at this point she wasn't the slightest bit hesitant about leaving him to do her job. The terrain was thick with brush and small rocky cliffs that the men had to find their way around. More than once,

Ember went into areas where Marcus and Victor couldn't, circling back each time.

Still, Marcus could not help but be frustrated by his own slow pace. He was used to being a leader when fighting fires, and here he was both leader and follower—with Ember covering ten times the ground he and Victor could.

Ember leaped onto a rocky ledge with a line of scrub trees and turned back, questioning. "Think we can make it up there?" Marcus asked. He wanted to, but the ledge looked pretty narrow . . . even from where he stood.

"Let's give it a shot," Victor answered. He looked around briefly. "I don't see a better route. You go ahead. I'll follow."

With another grunt, Marcus hauled himself up onto the wider end of the outcropping, using a scrub pine for support. To his left was a curving wall of rock interspersed with soil. A smattering of tiny trees and bushes poked their way between the rocks to sun and air. Marcus put one foot in front of the other, grasping scrub branches and rock protrusions and balancing as best he could. He could hear Victor behind him, while Ember, having seen them following, had cleared the ledge and was ranging on ahead and tracking like a pro.

"You good?" Marcus called back to Victor without turning around—the ledge was too narrow for that to be smart or safe.

"I'm still here, if that's what you . . . oh, crap!"

Marcus heard the rustle of a branch and then a series of expletives. Out of the corner of his eye, he saw a shape fall from the ledge and plummet twelve feet to the ground and land with a thud.

25

"Victor!" Marcus shouted, clutching the biggest pine branch his hand could find and turning his head as far as he could without turning his body and risking a fall himself.

"I'm here . . ." Victor moaned. "I'm down, but I'm here." He rolled onto his side and put his hands down for support to try to get to his feet. But the moment he put weight on his right leg, he winced and let out a yelp. "Ouch! Nope. Nope."

"That doesn't sound good," Marcus said. He was inching his way backward to get off the ledge and to

Victor, and trying not to hurry . . . two injuries would be a lot worse than one.

"It's not good." Victor's voice was full of remorse. "It's not good at all . . ."

Marcus took his last step off the ledge and recalled his partner. "Ember, come!"

"I twisted my knee pretty badly," Victor announced as Ember rounded a corner and bounded up to them. She knew right away that Victor was hurt, and gently pushed her muzzle into the hand that held his injured leg. "You're going to have to go ahead without me."

Though it wasn't what Marcus wanted to hear, he knew it was true. If Victor couldn't walk, he wouldn't be able to help—he'd be a burden. He got out his map and compass and compared it to the GPS. He was tempted to point out that a second source for location was useful in situations like these, but thought better of it. Victor's expression clearly revealed his regret.

Once he was clear about where they were, Marcus

spread out his map next to Victor to confirm and mark it. No matter how certain he thought he was, two heads were always better than one.

"Looks like we're right about here," Marcus said, pointing to a spot near the center of the map. "This is the ridge up ahead, here's the lake where we stopped, and this is the stream we crossed earlier . . ."

Victor nodded his agreement, unable to mask the pain his injury was causing, or his disappointment. He was devastated about letting his team down, but there was nothing to be done other than to call in his location and let Marcus and Ember go ahead while he waited for help to arrive.

"Yeah, that looks right." Victor placed his finger on the spot and compared it to the GPS. "Go ahead and call it in."

The radio crackled, and Marcus told Greta what had happened. "Ember and I will go ahead while Victor waits here. There are no hazards nearby, and I'm pinging it on both of our GPSs," he said.

"I don't think we can land a chopper there—it's too tight. We'll send a ground crew his way," Greta replied. "Use extra caution, Marcus. It's not entirely safe for you to go on alone."

"Absolutely will," Marcus replied, looking at Ember. He wasn't actually alone.

After signing off, he turned back to Victor, who had propped himself up against a rock and was going through his pack. "You going to be all right?" Marcus asked. "Do you have enough water? Food? Your bivvy in case you have to sleep out here?"

"I'm all set here," Victor assured him, patting his pack. "Just me and my GORP. Now please get on with your search so we can all get home safe, okay? I've cost us enough time."

Marcus's brow was furrowed, but he pulled the sock out of his pack and held it out to Ember, who licked Victor's hand in goodbye before returning to Marcus's side. She sniffed more lightly this time, and waited.

"Find!" Marcus said, repeating the command after her fresh whiff of the scent article. He was surprised to realize that his voice sounded tired. He felt tired, too. And not only had the search just started, it wasn't going as planned. He and Ember were moving on without Victor. But, Marcus reminded himself, they were still together and they were still on the trail of the hikers.

Ember took a longer, safer way back up to the ledge, and Marcus followed, waving to Victor. "I hope they get here soon, but if they don't, I know where you are," he called.

"Just go," Victor said, waving his bag of raisins and peanuts. "I'm fine."

Marcus reminded himself that it was still early in the day. There was plenty of daylight left, and the weather was clear . . . there was no rain or snow in the forecast. When he reached the end of the ledge, he turned and waved again, and then slipped out of sight.

In the distance, Marcus could see Ember's tail and nothing else. She was tracking with new purpose and seemed even more directed than before. With Victor down, Marcus felt uneasy. He had to work hard to keep himself in check—he didn't want to give Ember any signals that might confuse her. He took a deep breath when he spotted her circling back to him. She was getting close when she suddenly stopped and lifted her nose to the air, her ears tight against her golden head.

It was clear to Marcus that she smelled something . . . something she didn't like.

"What is it, girl?" Marcus asked. He raised his own nose and took a sniff but didn't smell anything . . . human noses were pathetic compared to dogs'.

Ember sniffed the air again and moved forward more slowly than before, her tail low.

About twenty minutes later, Marcus stopped in his own tracks—he could smell it now. Fire. He was reaching for his radio to update Incident Command when it crackled to life.

"We've just received word of a forest fire located at Box Canyon and moving west." Greta's voice was strong. "Helicopters will be dropping water to contain the spreading and cool the area enough for ground crews to get in. We've got you on the tracker, but don't want you getting too close. Keep us informed of the conditions. And Marcus, be conservative. This is a rescue mission, not a sacrifice . . ."

"Got it, over," Marcus said, holstering the radio. He checked his GPS, trying to determine how far he was from the fire. It looked like four miles. Between the mountains and the foliage, he couldn't see smoke or flames, but based on the information he had and the increasingly obvious smell of smoke, he suspected the fire was growing. The back of Marcus's neck prickled with worry as Ember returned to his side, whimpering.

"It's okay, girl," he reassured her. But was it? He buried his hand in her scruff, feeling her scar. Ember was a skilled tracker and a tireless worker, but would the smoke make it harder—or even impossible—to find the hikers? He wished that they had years of experience under their belts to help answer that question. But even if they did, they were in an active search situation. There was no way to know how it would turn out until it was over. That was simply the nature of the beast.

Marcus's thumb paused at the edge of Ember's scar, and the memory of when they first met flashed in his mind. He could practically feel her tiny, lifeless body in his hand . . . the rise of her fuzzy chest as he shared his breath.

Ember whimpered again, pulling him out of the memory. He looked down at her liquid brown eyes and asked a different, more concerning question.

Would being this close to a forest fire be so upsetting that Ember would fall apart? They'd already lost one member of their team to injury, and Marcus knew all too well that he couldn't find the hikers alone.

He felt a wave of panic as indecision overwhelmed him. He wanted to go on and turn back all at once.

But turning back was not an option.

26

The smell of smoke was all around and the light from the sun began to look burnished. Ember shook her head as if she could clear the smell from her nose, but it was pointless. The burning, smoky scent was everywhere. Fortunately she could still detect the smell from the sock. She hadn't lost the trail, and sensed that they were closer than ever. And more than ever, she wanted to "find."

The golden dog gazed at Marcus, who kept looking at the tiny screen he carried. He looked worried. He looked . . . uncertain.

Ember let out an impatient whine, and Marcus lifted his head.

"Ready, girl?" he asked, though he didn't have to. He could see she was ready, and clear. She had read his mind . . . and made it up for him. Her ears and tail were at attention. Her eyes were bright. She was determined!

"Okay." Marcus nodded, and Ember was off, moving with renewed energy and confidence.

"Maybe I should have named you Spark," he said, mostly to himself.

Marcus felt his own worries fade as he trailed after Ember, keeping a close eye on their GPS location. If she started toward the fire, he'd have to recall her.

The terrain flattened some and the smoke turned the sun an eerie reddish orange. Marcus's radio crackled with nonstop reports.

"This fire is serious," Greta's voice reported. As IC, she had to monitor everything that affected the mission, and that included weather, hazards in the search area, and now a fire. "It's growing fast and the winds are unpredictable."

Marcus didn't stop to respond. If the winds were making the fire unpredictable, they'd be making Ember's scent trail unpredictable, too. They had to keep moving.

The radio crackled again. "Marcus, I'm thinking about calling off the search."

There they were—the words Marcus suspected were coming but did not want to hear. He let them hang in the air momentarily before radioing back.

Whether to continue the search or not was not his call. That decision was entirely up to the incident commander, and for good reasons. The searchers in the field could be easily compromised by fatigue, hunger, or injury. Victor was a case in point.

At the same time, Marcus really wanted to see this search through. Ember was totally committed, and there were children involved. He also wanted his first real mission with Ember to be a success. "Greta, I think we're close."

A trickle of sweat ran down Marcus's back, giving him a shiver. The afternoon sun and heat from the fire were combining to make the air oppressive. He stifled a cough. It was getting thick with smoke as well. Unfortunately he hadn't thought to bring a mask.

Marcus stood still, waiting for the next radio crackle. Finally it came. "Proceed for now," Greta said. "But be prepared to be called off."

"Got it," Marcus replied. He holstered the radio. In the distance, he could make out the unmistakable low rumble of a fire consuming the woods, like an ominous hum. Tiny bits of ash were floating in the air, settling on the trees and ground around him. Marcus moved forward, keeping his steady pace. If Greta called them back, he would go—she was the incident commander, and she was in charge. As a firefighter, he could tell the fire was significant, and he knew he and Ember would be of no help to anyone if they became injured, or worse . . .

Taking a bandanna from his pack, Marcus dampened it with water from a water bottle and tied it over his nose and mouth. He took three long strides and crested a small hill in time to see Ember disappear over the next one, ears and tail at attention. She reappeared quickly, lingered to sniff carefully, then took off on a new trajectory—toward the fire.

"Oh, Ember, are you sure?" Marcus whispered to himself, knowing full well that she was. The golden Lab looked back at Marcus, pausing for a split second before turning again and taking off at a run.

Yes, she was sure. Yes, the hikers were in the same direction as the fire. And yes, she wanted to find them!

27

Marcus touched the radio on his belt but did not remove it. He looked ahead, toward the wide funnel of smoke rising into the air. He blinked several times. His eyes stung. Through the thickening smoke, he saw Ember still moving forward with determination.

Ember drew in air. The smoke was nearly overpowering the scent of her target, making her slightly less sure of her direction. But she could still pick up the unique scent, and she was certain they were getting closer. She paused and lifted her snout. A whimper escaped her throat. The rumbling sound of the hungry fire, the acrid smell, the dark smoke. They weren't just threatening to drown out the scents she was trying to follow. They were dredging up memories. They reminded her of the time under the house, when she had to get her brothers and sisters out, when she could not find their mother. They reminded her of Marcus. She looked back over her shoulder and caught her handler's scent. He was behind her moving steadily, if slowly.

She paused again as an impulse to run back to Marcus's side came over her. She was especially reluctant to get too far ahead of her partner since Victor was no longer with them. But she remembered her training. She could, and should, range out of sight of Marcus. She was faster on her own. She gave one last backward glance and refocused on her goal.

Marcus saw Ember look back, and then she put on a burst of speed. He tried to pick up his own pace, anxious to be closer to her the nearer they got to the fire. Greta could call them off at any moment. They did not have much time—nor did the hikers . . . if they were out here. He hoped Ember's renewed energy meant that she knew something he did not.

Pausing, Marcus listened for Ember's alert. The only thing he heard was the roar of the forest fire getting louder, and another sound that would only make things worse: the wind. It was blowing up the ridge. It was good that it wasn't blowing the fire toward them, but it would fan the flames nonetheless.

Fighting back a cough, Marcus touched his radio again. He should report the weather to his IC. The conditions were getting more treacherous with each passing minute. But just then he heard the sound he'd been straining to hear: three short, sharp barks. Ember had found the hikers!

The barks were close, and they gave Marcus strength. He surged up the hill toward the sound. There was not a moment to lose. Shouldering his way through some brush, he stopped short.

Ember was sitting by the two missing girls on the

edge of a drop-off. When Marcus came into view, Ember stood up ,and barked again. The girls also stood and both began shouting at once.

"Our daddy! He's down there!" The taller girl pointed toward the precipice, her dirty face streaked pink with trails left by her tears.

"He needs help," the smaller girl added, tugging on Marcus's arm and drawing him closer to the edge of the cliff. "He's hurt!" Her tear-streaked cheeks matched her sister's.

Marcus could see that the girls were frantic with worry, and understood why. They'd been alone up here for more than a day, probably with very little to eat or drink, worrying about their dad in the giant rock crevice, and smelling the approaching fire. He pulled the handkerchief away from his mouth.

"I'm going to help your dad," he said reassuringly. "But I need you both to listen to me, okay?"

The smaller girl nodded and wiped her nose with

the back of her hand. It was covered in soot and snot. "Okay."

"Great. Can you tell me your names?"

The older girl spoke first. "I'm Rachel, and this is Olive."

Marcus held out a hand. "Nice to meet you, Rachel. Olive. My name is Marcus, and this is Ember."

Ember licked each of the girls' hands in greeting, and Olive giggled.

"The first thing I need you to do is come away from that ledge," Marcus told them firmly. He needed both of them to listen, and there was no time to waste.

Rachel looked doubtful. "But our daddy is down there!" she said. "He can't get out!"

The back of Marcus's throat spasmed, and he coughed violently. The smoke was getting thicker. "I know," he wheezed. "And I'm going to get him out. But I need space to work, and I need to know you are both safe while I do it."

Rachel took another worried look into the crevice, and then relented. "Okay," she said shakily.

"Olive, can you hold on to Ember's collar for me?"

Olive nodded and grasped the collar while Marcus led the girls over to a small tree, settling them at the base of the trunk. Ember sat down between the two girls, and Olive slung an arm around the dog's back. "Ember is very smart and is trained to help in situations like these. She'll stay with you while I help your dad. Can you tell me your dad's name?"

"Travis. Our daddy's name is Travis." Olive barely got the words out before she started to cough. Marcus could see that they both had watery eyes . . . the smoke was choking.

Marcus pulled an extra shirt from his pack and wet both sleeves with fresh water. "Hold this over your mouth and nose. It'll make it easier to breathe." The girls each took a sleeve and did as instructed. Rachel put her other arm around her little sister, who was still leaning against Ember.

With the girls settled, Marcus pulled his handkerchief back over his nose and mouth and approached the ledge a second time. When he was still several feet away, he got down on his belly and scooted closer until he could see over the edge. The man below looked to be in his forties. He was dressed in hiking gear and lying on a ledge about twenty feet below. He raised an arm when he saw Marcus's face appear, and Marcus heaved a huge sigh of relief. He was conscious! His job just got a hundred times easier.

"Travis, can you hear me?" Marcus called.

"I can hear you. Are my girls okay?"

"Yes," Marcus confirmed. "The girls are fine. I'm Marcus Riley, and I'm trained in search and rescue." He introduced himself before informing Travis about the next, crucial steps. "We need to get you all out of here as quickly as we can. There's a fire to the east of us that's spreading. Are you injured?" Marcus asked.

"My ankle," Travis shouted back. "I think it's broken. I can't put any weight on it."

Marcus could see from twenty feet away that Travis's ankle was badly swollen, which explained why he hadn't been able to climb up after his fall off the rocky cliff. That, and the fact that it was practically vertical. It would be a challenge to get him up with assistance, but it was not insurmountable.

"I'm going to be out of view while I get situated to help you out of there, okay?"

Travis nodded. "Yes, okay. I'll just hang out down here . . ."

Marcus half smiled. Travis still had a bit of a sense of humor, which was a good sign. He commando-crawled back from the ledge and unclipped his radio. "We've found them!" he reported to IC. "We are with them now."

"Good job!" Greta radioed back, though Marcus knew her well enough to hear that she wasn't entirely relieved. Marcus reported the details and his plan to get Travis back on the trail.

"I'm sending a chopper," Greta said. "Even if Travis

can walk, you can't hike out with this smoke. I have your location. Let me know when you've secured the victim."

"Will do," Marcus replied, and holstered his radio. He glanced at Ember and the girls, and couldn't help but notice the ash falling on and around them like grim snow. Olive was completely slumped against Ember and looking drowsy. She probably hadn't slept at all the night before. They'd been through an ordeal, and it wasn't over yet.

Marcus pulled off his pack and opened it, digging around until he found a long piece of webbing. Since Travis looked to be a bit smaller than he was, Marcus used the length of his own arms to measure a loop and then adjusted accordingly. He tied an overhand knot several inches from one end and threaded the other end through. Then he attached a carabiner and a rope to the makeshift harness and crawled back to the edge.

"I'm sending down a harness," he shouted. Travis looked up and nodded. He caught the descending piece of webbing and untied it from the rope used to lower it. Marcus explained how to put the loop behind his back and thread it through his legs, and then pass the ends back through the loop before tying it around his waist and securing it with the carabiner.

"Next I need you to thread the end of the rope through the figure eight that's already there on one end," he instructed. "And make sure the tail is about eight inches long so it won't untie."

Travis completed the task quickly and looked up, ready for more instructions. "You're taking me back to my rock climbing days," he called.

Marcus, who wished he could secure the harness on the victim himself, was more than a little relieved to hear that Travis knew a bit about knots. "Hang tight!" he called down. He crawled back from the ledge and found a scrub pine with a sturdy trunk to use as an anchor, then attached a premade pulley with a strong braking system. When he was satisfied, he made his way back to the edge.

"Ready?" he called.

"Ready!" Travis replied.

Hand over hand, Marcus pulled the rope and Travis up the sheer wall. He could feel Travis helping as much as he could with one leg, but the going was slow. The strain made him cough, but he held tight to the rope.

Finally Travis's head appeared. He gripped the ledge and hoisted the rest of his body up before rolling onto his back in relief.

"Daddy!" the girls shrieked when they saw him. Marcus hurried to move him away from the drop-off as his girls rushed over to him for an ecstatic, three-way hug.

Ember wagged beside them, her tail low. She was happy to see the pack reunited, but she knew the danger was not over. They were not out of the woods and the fire was close. She sneezed, and ash flew out of her snout.

Too close.

28

"I'm all right," Travis assured his girls, squeezing them tight. "We are all right."

Olive was clinging to her dad and sobbing, her tears leaving fresh tracks down her soot-covered face. Travis held them both until they had calmed, then broke away and hopped over to Marcus. "Thank you," he said, offering a hand.

Marcus's face was serious as he signed off with Greta. "Don't thank us until it's over," he replied, quietly so as not to frighten the kids. "We're not out of danger yet." He handed Travis a wet cloth to breathe through and then took out his map, spread it on the ground, and studied it for a moment. It was so much easier to get the big picture of the terrain on paper as opposed to scrolling on a tiny screen. He put his finger on the spot where they were, then looked in ever-widening circles for a spot where a helicopter might be able to touch down. He knew Greta was likely doing the same thing back at base camp.

Unfortunately there was no large, flat place big enough for a chopper anywhere near them. And even if he miraculously found a flat space, it would be covered in trees, making it impossible for a helicopter to land.

His radio crackled, and the helicopter pilot confirmed from the air that he would not be able to land, and not only because of the tree-covered, steep terrain. "The heat and smoke from the fire are pummeling us," the pilot reported.

"Marcus, I need you to move farther away . . . to the west. Can you do that?"

Marcus looked at the exhausted girls and their little legs. He looked at Travis's swollen ankle. Neither looked promising, but what choice did they have?

"Yes," he said, and signed off.

Shouldering his pack, Marcus called to the rest of the group. "We've got to get farther away from the fire, and find a place where a chopper can land," he explained.

Ember looked at him, and Marcus swore she understood what he'd said. It wasn't a command she'd been taught, but Ember seemed to get it, anyway. She nudged the exhausted girls back the way they had come, sticking close for moral support. Marcus walked alongside Travis, supporting him on one side.

The going was slow.

Raising her nose but not stopping, Ember found

a path for the group to follow. She was not scenting a person, or even an object. She was following a path to cleaner air, a path away from the fire. After they'd gone about a hundred yards, she paused and looked back at Marcus, who nodded. "Keep going," he told her.

Rachel and Olive coughed through the shirtsleeves they still held to their faces. Ember stayed close, but two paws ahead, finding their path. She fought back an instinct deep inside—an impulse to run! She blinked her stinging eyes and tried not to focus on her burning snout as she continued onward. At last she heard something overhead, and stopped to listen over the wind and the low hum of fire. It was the *whop, whop, whop* of helicopter blades!

A fallen log lay across the path, and Ember jumped up onto it. She waited while the girls, and then Marcus and the man, crawled under. When they emerged on the other side, they were in a small clearing. It wasn't big enough for the chopper to land, but it was large enough and clear enough of trees for the pilot to drop a harness without it tangling.

The chopper dipped lower, blowing up dust and needles to mix with the smoke. It was difficult to hear, or see. Ember's ears lay tightly against her head.

Marcus helped Travis settle himself against the fallen log and took both Olive and Rachel by the hand, leading them to the center of the clearing. He caught the yellow harness as it came down. The girls would go first.

While he secured the wide yellow straps around them, Marcus explained what would happen. "We will use this to pull you up to the helicopter. These straps are very secure, so you will be totally safe. As soon as you are both inside the chopper, the pilot will lower the harness again for your dad, and then for me and Ember. Can you give me a thumbs-up?" he shouted over the din.

Squinting from the dust and smoke, the girls both gave him a thumbs-up. Marcus signaled to the pilot, and the girls were lifted off the ground. Olive shrieked in excitement and surprise, holding tight to her sister.

"You're doing great!" Marcus shouted up to them.

The girls were lifted higher and higher, and soon disappeared into the body of the chopper. A few moments later, the harness lowered again, and Marcus helped Travis into it, trying to breathe as slowly as he could behind his handkerchief. When Travis was safely inside the helicopter, the harness appeared a third time, and Marcus climbed in.

"Ember!" he called. She was at his side in an instant. Bending down, he slid a sling under her torso, fastened it at the top, and clipped it to his own harness.

Ember let her body relax. She remembered the sling from training—Marcus and Roxanne had raised and lowered her several times in strange places until she was comfortable going up and down. This was the first time she'd been lifted into a helicopter, but she did not doubt her handler. She trusted Marcus as much as she trusted herself.

Marcus and Ember swung in the air for several minutes, feet dangling, as they were lifted to the chopper. When they cleared the treetops, they saw the fire just over the next ridge, a jagged hot line belching black smoke that turned dark gray as it rose into the air. When they reached the helicopter, they were pulled inside the crowded cabin. Travis and his girls were smooshed into two seats in the back, clinging to one another. Marcus took the last seat and pulled his good dog into his lap, where she just barely fit.

Ember licked Marcus's dirty, salty, smoky cheek. "Thanks!" He laughed and ruffled her ears.

He understood the lick was his reward for a job well done, and now it was time for Ember's reward. Marcus reached into his vest pocket and pulled out his chewed-up glove. Ember snatched it and gave it a light chew. They couldn't play glove tug-of-war in the crowded helicopter, but Ember glowed just having it in her mouth.

"You did it, Em!" Marcus whispered in his dog's velvet ear. Her fur felt soft against his cheek. "We both did."

29

Curled on the truck seat next to Marcus, Ember opened her eyes. She stood up and stretched as best she could in the cab. They had been driving for a long time, and though Ember usually preferred to pass the time by snoozing, she'd gotten a smell in her nose while she was dozing. It was a smell that told her to get up before she missed something. The smell was familiar, and . . . Ember whined. The smell was *good*. Her mouth opened and she began to pant. She suddenly knew where they were. They were . . . *here*!

Marcus laughed as Ember paced the two steps back and forth on the seat and pushed her snout through the crack in the window to breathe the scent deeper into her nostrils.

"I know!" he said. "Exciting, huh?" The truck rolled to a stop, and Ember whimpered at the door while Marcus got out and walked to the passenger side. She could not wait to get out to see . . . *everyone*!

With a leap she was out on the pavement. She ran up the walk and stood wagging at the door to the Sterling Center.

"Hang on, I'm coming!" Marcus chuckled as he hurried to catch up. If he'd had a tail, it would be wagging, too. He turned the doorknob, and the two of them stepped inside the welcome center, where they were greeted by Shelby.

"Oh my gosh! Hi! What are you guys doing here?" she asked with a big smile. "I'd get up, but . . ." She pointed at the tiny dog with giant ears on her lap. The dog looked very much at home, and not at all like the usual Sterling pooch. Marcus raised his eyebrows in surprise.

"Is that a . . . Chihuahua?" he asked.

"Yeah!" Shelby said.

Marcus nodded in stunned silence. It was surprising to see a tiny pup at Sterling, and just as surprising to see a dog on Shelby's lap! Before Shelby could say another word, Morgan burst through the back door. She skidded to a halt when she saw who had just arrived, then ran full tilt toward Marcus and Ember with her arms flung wide.

"Ember!" After giving Marcus a quick squeeze, she dropped to her knees to look Ember in the eye and throw her arms around her neck. Ember wiggled away, too happy to hold still, and landed a sloppy kiss across Morgan's nose and mouth.

Morgan wiped the slobber off with the back of her arm, but was all smiles.

"We just came to say hello," Marcus said with a shrug and smile.

"Oh yes, you *have* to say hello." Morgan grabbed Marcus by the arm and yanked him out the back while Shelby rolled her eyes and waved them all goodbye.

"Just wait until Forrest sees you! He's gonna lose it!" Morgan was skipping, her dark eyes wide with excitement while she pulled. It reminded Marcus of the first time he met Morgan, when she dragged him to the canine pavilion to meet Ember. Marcus allowed himself to be hustled up the steps and into the Sterling residence.

"Look who's here!" Morgan shouted the moment the door was open.

She ushered Marcus and Ember down the long hall and into the dining room, where most of the Sterling clan were gathered for a Friday afternoon meeting.

Georgia was on her feet in an instant, sweeping her huge mass of hair over one shoulder before giving Marcus a hug and asking if he was hungry. "What a wonderful surprise!" She gestured toward a chair. "Please . . . sit."

Pedro and Roxanne, who were there for their weekly meeting, were surprised and happy to see one of their newest teams return.

Frances, who had only stopped by for coffee, beamed. "Always nice to see Sterling alumni." She took Marcus's large hand in hers. Her grip was surprisingly strong.

"We don't mean to interrupt," Marcus said.

"You're not interrupting. Sit, sit." Georgia insisted. She slipped Ember a dog treat, and the yellow Lab started making her rounds. She stopped at each chair for a sniff or a pat and leaned first into Roxanne, then Pedro, then Frances, then Georgia, and then Morgan before starting over again. It was only a matter of minutes before everyone's pant legs were covered in golden fur.

Things were finally sort of settled, and Marcus was

about to tell everyone about their first mission, when the back door opened and Forrest strolled in.

Ember was back on her feet and across the room in two bounds. She had missed that twelve-year-old-boy smell! She nearly tackled Forrest, who whooped in delight.

"Ember!" He'd been missing her as well. The two tussled for a minute, and then Forrest remembered to say hello to Marcus. They bumped fists, and Marcus ran his hand over his close-cropped hair. He dipped his chin at Forrest, who did the same. His curls were gone, and his hair was as close cut as Marcus's!

"Looking sharp," Marcus said.

Georgia laughed. "That's a lazy haircut," she teased, though she thought her boy looked handsome in his new do. "Now tell us, Marcus. What have you and Ember been up to?"

Marcus relayed the story of their mission to a rapt audience. There was hardly a sound in the dining room, save the swishing of Ember's tail on the hard-wood floor or a soft slurp as someone took a sip of coffee.

"We had to come and tell you in person," Marcus finished.

"Because Ember is a rock star!" Morgan shouted.

Marcus grinned. "If she is, it's because of all of you," he replied gratefully.

"Wait, you found the missing hikers during the Box Canyon fire last month?" Roxanne gasped. "That was you?"

"Yep." Marcus nodded proudly. "Well, it wasn't actually me. It was Ember."

Pedro shook his head, astounded. "I'm surprised the smoke and changing winds didn't throw her off . . . especially given her history."

Marcus reached down to pet his dog, who had finally settled near his feet after doing a couple more laps around the table. "She really held it together.

That family never would have made it without her. I was so proud. I still am."

"So am I!" Morgan stood up to get Ember another treat from the jar of biscuits they kept by the stove and was almost run over by Juniper.

The youngest Sterling came flying into the kitchen wearing a cat-ear headband and clutching a gray furry bundle to her chest.

"Please, Mom. Please, please, please!" Juniper begged, interrupting everything.

Georgia put her hand on her daughter's shoulder to get her to slow down. "Why don't you say hello to our guests, and then you can tell me why you are running in here full of pleases," she said calmly.

Juniper looked around the table, noticing the other people in the room for the first time. She said her hellos as Martin came in through the back door looking a little exasperated.

"Ember! Marcus! Good to see you." Martin shook

Marcus's hand and gave Ember a pat before sidling over to his wife and saying in a hushed tone, "I told her she had to clear it with you." He nodded toward Juniper, who opened her hands further to reveal Bud, the gray striped kitten.

"Clear what, exactly?" Georgia asked. Her hands found their way to her hips. She had a feeling she was about to get talked into something.

Twig came in the cat door and sidled over to Ember. He greeted her by touching his nose to hers and then leaped on the counter to be part of the conversation.

"I want to keep him," Juniper said, looking up at her mom with pleading eyes.

"He's the last one," Martin explained gently. "We just adopted out Scratch."

"And Bud's my favorite!" Juniper exclaimed. "After you, Twig," she added quickly.

Georgia and Martin looked at each other, already knowing the answer was yes.

"Okay, but—" Georgia tried to launch into a quick speech about the responsibility involved in caring for another animal, but Juniper was already bolting for the door.

"Thank you, thank you, thank you!" She beamed at her parents like a flashlight. "We have to get started on training right away!" she said over her shoulder before the door shut behind her. "I think Bud has got what it takes to be a real SAR cat!"

Everyone at the table laughed. Martin stroked Twig's back, and the grouchy cat leaned into his palm. "Looks like you're off the hook, Twig! But don't fret. Not every animal is rescue material," he joked.

Marcus silently agreed. He reached down to rest his hand on Ember's glowing fur. Not every animal had what it took. Luckily for both of them, Ember definitely did.

A NOTE FROM
THE AUTHORS

As bona fide dog lovers we jumped at the opportunity to write stories about rescue dogs. Knowing that
the project would require extensive research, we excitedly explored websites, books, articles, and anything
else that could help us learn about rescue dog training, handler pairing, and the disasters dogs assist
with. We found dozens of inspiring stories about real
dogs doing what they do best: acting selflessly, loy-
ally, enthusiastically, tirelessly, and heroically to save
people in peril. We were won over by these incredible
tales of canines and their companions, and inspired

by the dedication and hard work so many two- and four-legged creatures undertake in service of others. We also learned that there are many differing theories and methods of dog training.

It can take years of training and discipline to develop dogs' natural gifts into skills that make them both safe and effective helpers in the aftermath of disasters. Dozens of canine search-and-rescue agencies all over the world do this important work, and while they all share the common goal of creating well-matched and successful dog and handler teams, each has its own philosophy and style. There is no single path to becoming a certified search dog. Though we were particularly inspired by the National Disaster Search Dog Foundation, established by Wilma Melville and her Labrador, Murphy, we pulled from several schools of thought regarding both training and searching to create these dog-inspired fictional stories. We hope you enjoy them. Woof!

ABOUT THE AUTHORS

Jane B. Mason and Sarah Hines Stephens are co-authors of several middle-grade novels, including the A Dog and His Girl Mysteries series and the Candy Apple titles *The Sister Switch* and *Snowfall Surprise*. As Sarah Jane they wrote the critically acclaimed *Maiden Voyage: A Titanic Story*.